CU00809896

John Storey is an award
academic books, some
translated into nineteen
is his first work of fiction. He is currently working on a
second novel called *To Fetch a Pail of Water.*

THE
DROWNING
MAN

JOHN STOREY

Northodox Press Ltd
Maiden Greve, Malton,
North Yorkshire, YO17 7BE

This edition 2024

1
First published in Great Britain by
Northodox Press Ltd 2024

ISBN: 978-1-915179-35-7

This book is set in Caslon Pro Std

For Timothy Digby

Rain, rain go away
Come again another day.
Rain, rain go away
Little Tommy wants to play.

Traditional nursery rhyme

Prologue

Parking the car next to Platt Fields, Tom listened as the police siren gave way to a song on the radio. He listened and heard his own voice singing the words. Singing along as if these were his words; as if these words were a commentary on everything that he had done and seen; a commentary on everything that had gone wrong; a commentary on every fatal mistake he had made. Baffled by his own incompetence, he wondered at what he had really done. He sang loudly, desperately, and opened the window to allow the rain to join with his performance. From Platt Fields he was accompanied by the struggling whines and whistles of a lone starling.

Tom saw the badly painted sky, dripping out of shape, and then he saw the man, as liquid as the water running down the windscreen. The man walked by and almost stopped, looking at him singing along, alone, loudly to a song on the radio. Tom turned off the car's engine and the music stopped. He was trying not to think, trying not to remember, when the man returned. This time he was on the driver's side. He leaned in through the open window, and in a sudden flash of light, turning quickly from white to grey, Tom felt a slash that burst open his throat. His eyes widened and then closed. His heart was banging like an unlocked door in the wind. He tried to undo his seat belt. He tried to stand up. But he could not do very much at all. He was shaking. He was wet. He was gasping for air. He was a drowning man.

Chapter One

'My name is Professor Brian Fish. I do hope you can help me.'

He said all this while stretching out his left hand. We shook hands and we both sat down.

I was surprised by his appearance. I'd remembered Fish as a man in tailored suits, expensive cotton shirts and what I'd always assumed was his old school tie. Here, he was dressed casually in jeans, suede boots, and a large woollen sweater. What hadn't changed were his boyish good looks. I calculated that he must be fifty-two, maybe fifty-three, but he looked like a man in his late thirties. He looked younger than he had when I'd been a student over a decade earlier.

'Hello. I'm Tom Renfield,' I said a little nervously.

He handed me his business card. I read it quickly before placing it in my in-tray. Professor Brian Fish, BA (Hons), MA, PhD. Professor of English Studies. Etc., etc.

I handed Fish my business card. He accepted it with two fingers and slowly shuffled it into the palm of his hand. He then placed it on the table and flicked it over. He stared at it for a moment and then flicked it over again. He looked up smiling. He held up my card and read it out loud: 'Tom Renfield. Private Investigator.'

He waited for a moment.

'Yes. I know who you are. You graduated from the university about ten or so years ago. How are you, Tom? Nice place. Your own?'

'No. I share it with another investigator.'

I felt a little wave of embarrassment using the word 'investigator.'

'Do I know him? Was he also a student of mine?'

Fish spoke with an accustomed authority. The words were delivered with a colonising wave of his right arm.

I carefully controlled my voice. 'My partner's a woman. She wasn't a student at the Met.'

Fish ignored my discomfort. 'Ah well, never mind.'

'What can I do for you, Professor Fish?'

'Please, call me Brian.'

'Okay.'

'It's nothing, really. I want you to locate somebody. She's a student. She has gone missing. You do that kind of thing, yes?'

'Yes, of course. I will need some details.'

I tried not to sound disappointed. I knew that missing person cases could be very unrewarding. Most people who disappear do not want to be found. But working for the university via Fish might increase our client base. So, I tried hard to be encouraged by what the case might offer. I was also a little flattered that Fish had asked me for help.

'Her name's Rebecca Morney. She's a final year student, a very good student, who has had a few problems recently. I've written down some details.'

Fish handed me a large manila envelope. Inside I found a sheet of paper and a photograph. The paper was a photocopied sheet of information about Rebecca Morney. It was obviously part of an official file he had obtained from Student Records. Fish had added a few handwritten notes. He had also crossed out her printed address and written a large question mark in the paragraph. The photograph was very different. Not the kind of photograph one would normally expect to be attached to an official file - not even a university official file.

She was leaning back against a short metal fence in a busy city street. Behind her, slightly blurred, there were traffic and pedestrians. I thought I recognised the location as the junction of Market Street and Deansgate. But the photograph had been cropped too tightly for me to be sure. The brightness suggested it had been taken during the summer. The amount of traffic seemed to indicate it had been taken in the late afternoon.

She was tall and slim, skinny almost. She wore a long, baggy black sweater and tight white jeans. One of her shoulders showed bare. Her hair was thick and dark brown, tied behind. She had thick eyebrows, very dark.

She stared at the camera with a rather gloomy faraway look in her eyes. Dark and misty, gleaming in her pale face. There was a hint of sleeplessness in and under them. But they were very beautiful eyes. I wondered who had taken the photograph and how had it come into Fish's possession.

I tested the water. 'This is an unusual photograph for an official file.'

Fish didn't respond. Instead, his eyes scanned my office.

I tried a different approach. 'Did you take this photograph?' I asked as casually as I could.

'No. Of course not.'

'How did it come into your possession?' I had spoken a little too quickly. Fish pretended not to have observed my hurry or my rather abrupt tone. What he was not used to, he probably did not notice.

Fish continued slowly with great assurance. 'She must have left it by mistake in my office after an essay tutorial. I found it on my desk one day and never got around to giving it back. You can return it when you find her, Tom.'

He laughed softly and gently. I assumed he was amused by the absurdity of my suggestion that he might have taken the photograph. Or perhaps he was laughing at the absurdity of a former student asking such a question?

I quickly got back on track. I composed myself and formulated another question. I tried very hard not to appear rude. 'May I ask why you want me to find her? Why not go to the police? They do this kind of thing all the time. They are set up for it. And they don't charge sixty pounds a day, plus expenses.'

The last sentence I regretted immediately. It sounded like a quotation from a novel. I worried my face might be going a little red.

Fish smiled. 'The police?' He thought for a moment. 'It's too early to involve the police. They would make too much fuss. The police are too public. Once one involves them one cannot tell them to stop. No, it is not yet the time for the police.'

He was probably thinking that a private detective could be hired and fired without awkward questions being asked. I suppose that's our appeal. We do what we are asked to do, when we are asked to do it. The client remains in control. And we get paid, so I shouldn't sound so troubled by it.

'Besides,' he continued, 'involving the police might make matters worse.'

'In what way?' I inquired.

'It would look too heavy-handed. They would ask lots of awkward questions. If she is just being a *student*, I would look rather foolish. No, I think it is best if this is a private investigation. If necessary, the police can get involved later.'

There was another awkward question I had to ask. I secretly took a deep breath and then I asked it. 'Why are you involved?' The words seemed to take forever to form outside my mouth. 'I mean why are you personally involved, rather than the university? Surely this is a matter for them?'

'Well, it's rather silly really,' he replied with great confidence and authority. 'About two months ago she came to see me with personal problems. You know, as her personal tutor, she thought I might be able to resolve them. Well, I did my best and things did seem to settle down. I'm just a little worried that her problems may have surfaced again. You see, finals are coming up and she's a very bright student. I don't want her to mess up her degree. You know, ruin her life over some stupidity that is not as important as she seems to think it is.'

Fish turned his head to the open window. He seemed suddenly distracted by the noise outside. Before I could suggest I close it, he became focused again.

'You see, she's had a few problems. I've seen her a few times. I'm a bit worried something might have happened. Then again, I might be overreacting. You know what students are like. The police seem somewhat unnecessary now. That's why I'd like you to make a few discrete inquiries. Would that be possible?'

I nodded and smiled.

'This is all off the record, you understand. I don't want colleagues thinking I'm getting soft or sentimental, or anything like that. You understand?

'That is not an uncommon way of working,' I said, never having worked in that way before.

'You'll keep all this to yourself?'

'I'm a private detective,' I said, pretending to laugh.

'A private eye?'

'Yes.'

Fish moved his hand solemnly, first to his chest and then to his right eye. 'A private I or a private eye? Perhaps both?'

He laughed very loudly. Fish making jokes with an expectation of laughter was the Fish I remembered from twelve years earlier. But I was suddenly caught by the prospect of a case that might prove more interesting than all the insurance work I had been doing recently.

'Can I count on you, Tom?'

I felt like I was back in university again.

'Do you want me to start straightaway?'

'Yes. As soon as you can.'

'Do you have any thoughts about why she might have disappeared?'

'Well, as I said, she's had a few problems.'

'What kind of problems?'

'You know, the usual ones: girl student, never been away from home before. I'm sure I don't have to draw you a map. You were a student. You must remember what it's like?'

'Can you give me any details? Any names? That kind of thing.'

7

'It's difficult.'

Struggling against the feeling of being back in the university, I tried to be very professional. 'If I'm going to help, I need to know what you know. If you know anything at all, please tell me. You must tell me everything you know. It will make things easier.'

He responded calmly to what suddenly seemed my preposterous demands. He nodded, smiled, and looked away. Despite his calmness, it was obvious that he wasn't used to being spoken to in this way. He got up and walked to the window. He looked down at the street below. Without saying anything, or even looking in my direction, he returned to his seat. Fish sat in silence, appearing to think something over.

Again, I tried to soften my approach while remaining professional. 'Look, I don't mean to be rude, but you've asked me to find her. If I'm to be successful in this, I need to know anything that you know that is or might be relevant.'

Fish seemed casually reassured. He was back in a place he recognised. He thought for a moment, then glanced around the office. I watched him as I listened to the traffic, the construction work and the sound of blurred voices bubbling up from the street below. He was smiling now, and looked very relaxed. I didn't speak. I knew I was expected to wait.

'I suppose I'll have to tell you. It doesn't give me any pleasure. You must promise me that this information is handled sensitively. It's very difficult to speak badly about a colleague. Do you remember Bill Warner? He teaches English, the novel mostly, nineteenth-century stuff. Very boring, really. I'm sure you remember, Tom.' He paused for a moment. 'I'm sorry, I shouldn't say such things. Anyway, you know what I mean. You've met him. Worse, you were probably taught by him.'

He controlled a hollow laugh.

I conjured up a mental image of Bill Warner, a monotonous voice at the front of a lecture theatre. A man standing alone in a brown sports jacket, brown corduroy trousers, and sensible shoes, brown, holding on for dear life to a lectern as he time-travelled back to the nineteenth century.

I nodded and tried hard not to smile. I was a little embarrassed by my complicity.

'This is difficult. Well, I suppose I must. Warner was having an affair with Rebecca Morney. They were having an affair, I mean.'

Fish's voice trailed off abstractedly. He stared around the office again. He seemed to be looking for something.

'In fact, Rebecca Morney told me they were having an affair. She wanted to end it, but Warner was being difficult. I'm just worried that one of them may have done something silly. I really need to know whether that man's actions threaten to bring the School of English Studies into disrepute.'

I was still puzzled why this was something that Fish would concern himself with. He noticed my puzzlement and decided to explain.

'I am hoping to be Director of the School very soon, and more - a Deanship is almost a certainty - and I do not want my improved circumstances to start with a scandal.'

I nodded and smiled, unsure quite how to respond.

'You must remember Warner, Tom?'

The tone of the questions made it very clear that Fish did not think much of him. But I knew that already. He had not been afraid to ridicule and dismiss Warner when I had studied at the Met. This was probably very unprofessional, but to students it was also very amusing.

'He was okay,' I said, without much conviction.

'He's a footnote fetishist. He's never done anything but fucking footnotes.'

Fish's swearing, or at least the emphasis the word was given, surprised me. What I remembered was just ridicule, but this seemed like genuine anger. I smiled involuntarily, trying to visualise Warner copulating with a footnote. I was a student again. I needed to get back in the room, get back on the case.

Fish laughed to himself. He laughed very loudly, rocking in his chair.

'What sort of degree did you get?'

'First Class Honours.'

I said it too quickly; too precisely. I sounded too pleased with myself. Here I was aligning myself with Fish's small circle of those who deserved to be educated. It was not how I thought, so I was embarrassed to have said it.

'Good. Richly deserved. Well done. I mean, very well done, Tom.'

Fish's congratulations made me feel worse. These were the same words, word for word, that Fish had said to me twelve years earlier. I had been flattered then. Now I just felt irritated with myself. But I had remembered the words, the congratulatory words of the great man. They had obviously made a deep impression. I felt even worse.

'Warner's not in your league. A Lower Second from some backwater institution in Wales, the University of Dylan Thomas' Arse. How that man ever got a job at Manchester Met, I'll never know.' He said Manchester Met as if he was talking about his old Oxford college. 'And now this,' he added slowly and venomously.

Fish scrutinised the office again to satisfy himself that it did indeed represent the just rewards of a First-Class Honours degree. He picked up my collection of pencils. He seemed to count them before returning the mug to my desk.

'I wanted you because you are familiar with life at the university. Everyone in the School knows you are a private detective. In fact, you're something of a celebrity at open days. You know, telling potential students how well old students are doing. Private detective adds a little spice to an otherwise predictable list of civil servants, social workers, journalists, teachers, postgrads, etc.'

He paused for a moment, as if suddenly encountering unfamiliar terrain.

Chapter Two

Tuesday morning.

Another rainy day in Manchester, the words formed like the beginning of a song. I crossed All Saints Park, inhaling the fresh morning air deeply. Despite the drizzle, there were already students celebrating the first all-race elections in South Africa. I remembered the weather forecaster's words: 'Sunny spells developing later.' It seemed prophetic. I really hoped so.

I had a vague feeling of alienation as I made my way along the main corridor. Everything was the same and yet strangely different. I recognised certain faces, which in turn seemed to recognise me. But the recognition was never enough to solicit a welcome, or a polite word of hello or an offer of help. It was no longer my world. It had been the focus of my life - it had *been* my life - for three years. But now the buildings just made me feel uneasy, out of place. It was as if I had had my turn and now it was the time of others, unknown others who might resent my presence cluttering up the building with fragments of its past. I quickened my pace. I was glad when I reached Dr Warner's office.

Warner had seemed reluctant to commit to a meeting with me when we had spoken over the telephone. Eventually, I lied and said I was acting on behalf of Rebecca Morney's parents.

As I knocked, I was overcome with an increased sense of anxiety. What if Warner remembered me? It would make things a great deal simpler if he saw me only as a private detective. Outside his door I felt I was dissolving: my professionalism was melting away to reveal just another anxious student waiting for a verdict on work that should have been better. I took a deep breath and knocked loudly on the door. A rather nervous voice invited me to enter.

'Good morning, Mr. Renfield. We will have to be a fairly quick, as I'm doing a seminar in about twenty minutes, and I need a little time to prepare a few things. I cannot arrive unprepared. As I'm sure you can imagine, that would be very unprofessional.'

He had a way of speaking that produced an unintended comic effect.

I watched him force a smile. He looked just as I remembered him: a man in his late forties. Brown cord trousers, tweed jacket, checked shirt, dickie-bow, and sensible brown shoes, as my mum would have described them.

'There is little I can tell you, anyway. I'm not the best one to talk to about Rebecca Morney. I hardly know her. She's just one of many students. There are so many these days.' He spoke quickly and nervously, as if from a recently learned script.

He then fell silent. I had learned long ago that the silences between words were something to manage. I now knew that waiting without speaking often produced words that were not intended; words that slipped out despite an attempt to control their articulation. I just waited for Warner to begin speaking again.

I glanced around the room. On the two walls between window and door there were four or five paintings of rural scenes. Carefully framed reproductions. Yellow and green landscapes, mostly with rural labourers, men, women, and children, all looking so very happy and so very content. The past is a wonderful place. It is not just that they do things differently there, it is more that we insist they do.

Another print seemed out of place. It was a painting of Adam and Eve in the Garden of Eden. She had an apple in one hand and was picking another. Adam looked completely lost. A serpent, in almost human form, looked at Eve. What was strange was that

Adam and Eve seemed to be looking at someone on their left-hand side, outside the frame of the painting. For some reason I found the image slightly disturbing. Warner noticed my interest and offered an explanation that did nothing to ease my discomfort.

'It is a painting by the Flemish artist Hugo Van der Goes. It is called *The Fall* and was painted around 1479.'

I didn't want it to become a lecture, so I simply said, 'Interesting painting.'

'Very interesting,' he responded, resting his left hand on his large wooden table, close to a small leather-bound Bible. His table was a jumble of papers and books. Some of the books were opened, bookmarked with pens and pencils. There were scraps of paper everywhere. I almost envied his clutter.

'What exactly do you want to know?'

'I just want to ask you a few questions about Rebecca Morney. It won't take long.'

I wanted to keep the tone business like. My work had taught me that most people like talking more than they like listening. The less I said, the more I was likely to be told. The logic was obvious. But the practice was less straightforward. Stay quiet and listen. Just listen. But sometimes the nervous strain could be overwhelming.

He sat on the very edge of the chair, his feet beating out a slow, primitive dance movement on the floor. His unease was palpable. He removed a handkerchief from his left pocket and twisted it between the fingers of both hands. While he looked at the handkerchief, I looked at him. His head moved in and out of the frame of Van der Goes' painting. I was remembering something I had once heard Fish say about Warner. He was the kind of man who would buy an all-day ticket and then sit on the bus for the whole day, and boast about how much money he had saved. I had to suppress a smile, wondering why Fish had said it, and why I still remembered. It had never occurred to me to wonder if the story was true.

Warner leaned forward, his hands in his lap. He looked like he was preparing to talk to his knees. He opened his mouth to say something but changed his mind. He thought a little more and then said, 'There's not much I can tell you. She was a student of mine. She attended lectures and seminars. She always turned up for tutorials. Not the most able of students, but very willing. She was enthusiastic and polite. She attended everything she was supposed to attend. That's about it, I suppose. I'm sorry I can't tell you more, Mr Renfield.'

'What sort of person is she?' I said, ignoring his attempt to end the conversation.

'I've told you, attended well, enthusiastic.'

'No, I mean what is she like as a person. Not what kind of student is she.'

'I'm afraid I can't answer that kind of question. You see I only knew her as a student. Ours was a purely professional relationship. You will have to ask her friends.'

The words seemed too fluent, almost rehearsed. He moved some papers across his desk. It almost seemed as if he was deliberately obscuring the title of a book. He let his left-hand rest on the keyboard of his old Amstrad word processor. Was he thinking of typing a confession? Was there a confession already waiting to be printed? *If only*, I thought.

A moment more of edgy silence, then Warner spoke again. Slowly at first, lacking conviction. 'As I explained on the phone, I am not her personal tutor, so why do you want to speak to me about her disappearance? You should speak to her personal tutor.'

Warner seemed vulnerable, even a little stupid. He didn't respond to the question. Instead, he again moved some papers across his desk. He opened a book and then closed it. I noticed the title: *Mansfield Park*. Was it significant? Probably not. However, holding the book gave him confidence. He now spoke with more authority.

'Why do you wish to speak to me about Rebecca Morney? I've told you I am not her personal tutor. Speak to Ester Smith.

Dr Ester Smith is Rebecca's personal tutor. She'll probably be able to help. I'm sure she'll be very helpful. Would you like me to arrange an appointment?'

He put the book down on the table.

I wanted to ask him about what Fish had told me. I hesitated for a moment, unsure what to do. I decided it might be better to pretend I didn't know. That way I might learn more. If I simply came out with it, he may feel he is under attack and close all communications.

'Oh yes. I almost forgot,' he began again, in an apparent attempt to lighten the mood, 'she's writing a book on Lacan and detective fiction. Do you know the work of Jacques Lacan, the French psychoanalyst?'

I nodded and smiled, 'Yes, I have read some things by him.'

'Oh,' he said, a little surprised. 'Rather you than me. Anyway, the lecture might be good. You should talk to her about it. If she can't help you, you might be able to help her. You won't have had a wasted visit.'

Warner forced a smile. There was silence for a few moments. He appeared to be thinking about something. Talking about Rebecca Morney was obviously difficult for him. I waited. I let my eyes roll over the bookcase. It contained mostly nineteenth-century novels. I knew most of them. They brought back memories. My fingers moved over the spine of Mrs. Gaskell's *North and South*. I noted that there was nothing in the way of theory on his shelf. Warner and Fish were quite different literary academics.

He noticed my interest in the novel. He suddenly acknowledged that he remembered me as a student. This gave him renewed confidence. His demeanour lightened. His posture seemed to suddenly straighten, making him seem slimmer and taller, and younger. He smiled and fixed me with a very determined gaze. He straightened his dickie-bow. I was now in a context that reassured him, a context in which he knew who he was. Appropriate power relations were now in play.

Smiling, but in a serious sort of way, he changed the subject. 'It's just not the same as it was when you read English, Tom. It is Tom, isn't it?'

I nodded and said yes.

'It's all literary and cultural theory now. Oh, and that awful deadening cultural studies. It's the fault of people like Fish and, I suppose, to a lesser extent, people like Ester Smith.'

He thought for a moment.

'Okay, she's a theorist. But she's also a real scholar, a genuine literary scholar. She doesn't use theory to hide the fact that she doesn't really understand literature. Or know how to read it. She understands literature very well and she reads it very well.'

He paused briefly, as if to quickly refuel. He frowned and waited, slowly formulating his sentences, and I could tell they were going to be sentences. His frown gradually changed to a smile, a smile that almost became a laugh.

'No, it's all changed since your time here. These days, if you pull up someone for plagiarism, they tell you it's just an example of postmodern intertextuality. Or they say they are just being an active reader of other texts. Not books, mind. There are no books anymore,' he said pointing to his bookcase. 'There are no authors anymore, just texts, texts, texts. Especially to blame is Fish's appalling little *textbook*.'

He slurred the final word of the sentence; and it was a sentence, severe and damning. Text. The word itself was the very battlefield on which he fought. He hesitated, straightening his body as straight as it would go. Then he said it, the title of Fish's appalling little textbook: '*Post-Structuralism, Postmodernism, Post-English Studies*. It is a set text for all English Studies students and I, for one, do not mind saying it, that dreadful little book has ruined *decent pedagogy* - and I make no apology for that phrase - in this so-called English Department.'

He removed *North and South* from the bookshelf, holding it in his left hand and fingering it with his right. He was now absolutely and essentially reassured.

'This is not a *text*,' he said, addressing the audience at an imaginary conference. 'This is not a text; this is a novel; a work of literature. It has an author. It has a narrative. It has a *meaning*.'

I smiled in an expected sort of way. To be honest, I felt a little embarrassed. Although I wanted to ask him many more questions, I was relieved when he opened the door.

'I'm afraid, Tom, I must now ask you to leave. There are things I must do,' he said rather pompously.

I reminded him about his offer to arrange a meeting with Dr Ester Smith. He smiled. He was relaxed now. The war was turning his way. The conference army had been converted. The appalling little textbook had been beaten into retreat. Total victory now seemed an absolute certainty.

'Yes. Of course.'

He picked up the phone and fixed a meeting for 3 o'clock that afternoon. Smiling, he said: 'She will see you in her office. Do you know where that is?'

I said I didn't. He gave me instructions and we said goodbye. I would have to speak to him again, but, hopefully, after speaking to others about Rebecca Morney, our next meeting might prove to be a more productive one.

The fresh air outside in the park made me smile. The rain had cleared. The sun was quickly drying out the grass. I sat on a bench in All Saints Park and I thought about what Warner had said. Was any of it helpful? Did it help in any way? Two gentlemen of the road, sitting on the damp grass nearby, shared a can of premium lager. It made me thirsty. I thought about the pub and then decided that drinking on the job was not a good idea. *Eighth Day* or the *Cornerhouse*? I decided that soup at the *Eighth Day* would not walk me into temptation. I liked the bar too much in the *Cornerhouse*. With my new resolve still in place, I walked across the park in the sunshine thinking about what Warner had said, and what he hadn't said, and what I hadn't asked.

Chapter Three

Later the same day.

I was early. I entered the university's Ormond Building. Dr Ester Smith was delivering her famous lecture on Jacques Lacan and detective fiction. I was intrigued enough to decide to enter quietly and take a seat as close to the back as possible. The lecture theatre was very full, but I found a seat about three rows from the back.

'How can we sum up the relationship between what Lacan has to say about psycho-social development and the processes and procedures of the detective novel?'

This was my first encounter with Dr Ester Smith. I had graduated before she arrived at the university. I was immediately impressed by her presence. She had an entertaining way of delivering the complexities of theory. Her audience were attentive and absorbed; all seemed to be writing with great urgency, worried that they might miss any of her explanations and arguments.

'Last week, you will recall, I spoke to you about what is called 'the ideology of romance.' You can find quotations and more information in the seminar booklet on page twenty-four.'

Dr Ester Smith removed her dark blue linen jacket and carefully placed it on the back of a chair next to the lectern. The conservatism of her outfit was in sharp contrast to the luminous pale purple shirt she was wearing. The shirt gripped her body tightly. Her trousers pressed against her hips and thighs. She had the figure of a model. I couldn't help thinking that there had not been any lecturers as attractive as Dr Ester

Smith when I had been a student at Manchester Met.

'In the mythical moment of plenitude, in the realm Lacan calls the Real, there is no clear distinction between subject and object. Our union with the mother is perfect and complete. Our sense of selfhood emerges later, through a process Lacan identifies as the mirror stage.'

I surveyed the ninety or so assembled students, heads down, intently taking notes. Perhaps some of them knew where to find Rebecca Morney? Better still, she might be here.

'The mirror stage is the moment when we first recognise ourselves in a mirror, real or imagined. On the basis of this recognition or, more properly speaking, misrecognition - not the self, but an image of the self - we begin to see ourselves as separate individuals, we begin to enter the realm Lacan calls the Imaginary.'

I was finding it increasingly difficult to concentrate. My head was too full of Rebecca Morney. Taking notes would help. But somehow, I just couldn't play the game anymore.

'The Symbolic is the realm of culture.'

I scanned the rows of forward-facing heads, bowed in concentration on Dr Ester Smith's lecture. Surely, one of these heads must contain the information I was seeking.

'I can only be 'I' in and through language. But when 'I' speak I am always different from the 'I' of whom I speak. Subjectivity is thus produced from the very processes of language, made and remade within its patterns and articulations, and not an essential pre-given of nature. Language produces our very subjectivity, and yet it is forever outside our sense of being, belonging to others in the same way as it belongs to us. I am 'I' when I speak to you and 'you' when you speak to me. It follows from this that our sense of being a unique individual is always somewhat fragile.'

She was smiling now. Her very own, rather less than fragile, sense of self clearly enjoyed the staging of its own fragility. Perhaps here was someone to compare with Fish. I smiled inwardly at the thought that I would soon be questioning her about Rebecca Morney's disappearance. If anyone could help, I was becoming increasingly convinced that person was Dr Ester Smith.

'Selfhood, experienced as full and whole, as an extension of the mother's body, fragments in the mirror and in language. To be ourselves we must break from the completion of the moment of plenitude. We must resign ourselves to the fact that we can never return there, that moment of perfect self-identity and self-completion. We have been banished forever from the 'full' possession of the mother's body and in to the 'empty' world of language. Gone forever, we will, nevertheless, spend the rest of our lives searching for it; always making do with substitute objects and displacement strategies, in a hopeless attempt to fill the emptiness at the core of our being.

'To paraphrase Terry Eagleton, who explains it so well (the full quotation is in your seminar booklet on page twenty-seven), it is an original lost object - the mother's body - that is the engine driving forward the narrative of our lives, forcing us to find substitutes for this lost object in an endless metonymic movement of desire.'

Dr Ester Smith paused, gripped the lectern, steadying herself for the final assault on the intellectual capacity of her audience. There was a very brief smile, and an increased flow of confidence, as her voice began again.

'The ideology of romance is as an example of this endless search. What we should understand by this term, is the way that romance as a material and discursive practice holds that 'love' is the ultimate solution to all our problems. Love makes us whole, it makes us full, it completes our being. Love, in effect, promises to return us to the blissful state of the moment of plenitude, warm and secure against the body of the mother. But above all, love is a substitute for the self-completion of the Real.

'On page twenty-eight of the seminar booklet you will find John Storey's brief Lacanian discussion of *Paris, Texas*. He reads key moments in Travis Henderson's story as attempts to return to the Real.

'Detective fiction works what we might think of as the same psycho-ideological terrain. At its heart is the promise of a solution. Detection always ends with a moment of completion, the putting together of all the clues. The crime is solved. The search is concluded. What was episodic is now whole. Once again, we experience the blissful moment of plenitude. But it is only a substitute amidst substitutes. The moment passes and we begin our search again. Desire is always driven by lack and the impossibility of ever satisfying the condition of lack.

'In seminars we will consider a number of detective novels in the light of this theoretical approach.'

Outside the lecture theatre I met Dr Trefor Trelawny. He addressed me as he might have addressed a student returning after the Easter vacation. Twelve years was suddenly made to seem like four weeks.

'How are you, Tom? Keeping well, I hope?' he said with a knowing smile. He had hardly changed in twelve years, with his Richard Burton voice and his Richard Harris good looks. This was not a description I had made up; it was something that was said once in a drama seminar by Dr Ella Jones, who clearly found Trelawny very attractive indeed. Lots of other things she said made this very clear.

I nodded and smiled and said all the things expected of me. He also nodded and smiled, and then very quickly got to the point: 'I've seen a lot of you lately. Is it a sudden bout of missing us, or what? I believe you're a detective now, a private detective. Working on a case that involves the university. Or a member of staff, perhaps?'

He spoke very quickly, as if he had to say everything at once. I watched his face as he asked his questions. My curiosity was aroused. This was only my second visit to the university in over a decade. But I played it cool. 'How are you, Dr Trelawny?' I said, offering my hand.

Trelawny took my hand and responded: 'Trefor. Please call me Trefor, Tom.'

I smiled and waited for Trefor to continue. There was a short embarrassing silence. Then Trefor continued, again with great confidence: 'Is it interesting being a private detective? I've always wanted to write detective novels. Maybe we could meet sometime for a drink, or a meal, and I could quiz you about the business. You know, do a little background research. I'm sure it would be of enormous help. Yes, we should do it.'

He smiled and then got back to the point: 'What brings you to the university?'

'I'm looking into the disappearance, or possible disappearance, of a student. A final year student,' I added.

'Sounds interesting,' he said in such a way as to reveal a sudden lack of interest. What ever had prompted his questions, it did not seem to be connected to Rebecca Morney's disappearance. Or was he a great deal cleverer than I had been led to believe by the content of his lectures? The voice of Richard Burton and the good looks of Richard Harris he may have, but he was an awful lecturer. Never has the work of James Joyce made so little sense.

I pressed him. 'Rebecca Morney. Do you know her?'

He considered for a moment. One of the books he was carrying fell to the floor. I looked down; it was *Grey Granite* by Lewis Grassic Gibbon. He bent down to pick it up, while saying sorry to no one in particular. Perhaps to the author himself.

'A final year student, you say? I may have taught her in the first year. The name sounds vaguely familiar. If it is important to your case, I could check my records?'

'I don't think it is that important.'

He sounded suddenly reassured.

'Anyway, interesting case, I'm sure. I'm certain you'll sort it out, Tom. We must have that drink sometime. Got to dash, doing a lecture on *The Dubliners*. Bye.'

There seemed to be a newly acquired sense of cheerfulness about his manner as I watched him hurry down the corridor, heading with his books and notes to the new refectory. He probably intended to rehearse his lecture over a plate of sausage and beans. He had been famous during my time at university for this meal, and for covering his beans in black pepper. The meal was always washed down with a small bottle of mineral water and a black tea. Unfortunately, there is nothing particularly suspicious in such a routine, I thought.

I knocked on Dr Ester Smith's office door.

'Yes, come in.'

'Hello, I'm Tom Renfield.'

'Yes, I know who you are. Do sit down, Mr. Renfield. Did you enjoy the lecture?'

My surprise was obvious. She waited a moment and then said: 'I saw you at the back of the lecture theatre. I know all my students. And, besides, Dr Warner told me you wanted to speak to me.'

I explained that I had found the lecture very interesting indeed. Close up she seemed much too young to be a lecturer. Her features were much finer and gentler than they had appeared from the back of the lecture theatre.

'I know all my students. Strangers stand out, especially ones I am expecting,' she explained again.

As she was talking, I noticed the large poster on the wall behind her desk, *Idle Talk Costs Lives*. Stamped in red over the four words was an address, 19 Berggasse.

'I only heard the last twenty minutes or so.'

'Strangers stand out, especially when they arrive late.'

She smiled, obviously expecting an apology.

'Sorry. But yes, I did enjoy the lecture. When I was a student here there wasn't much talk of Jacques Lacan. Or detective fiction, for that matter.'

She smiled again. 'What can I do for you, Mr Renfield?'

'Please, call me Tom.'

She smiled without encouragement.

'I'm making inquiries about Rebecca Morney,' I said, wishing I hadn't suggested she call me Tom.

Dr Ester Smith listened politely to my words, smiling occasionally, but with little enthusiasm. Unlike Trelawny, she drew clear boundaries between detective work and detective fiction.

Without waiting for me to conclude, she interrupted. 'It can be very difficult for female students. It can be overwhelming sometimes. There was one man at my previous university, he's left now - not before time, who was part of the problem. He should have been helped earlier. He derived a very particular and perverse pleasure from reading and marking student essays. It was the excess of it all, the language, the ideas. As he marked an essay, he would find himself becoming more and more aroused, sexually aroused, at the thought that female students were sending him coded messages. He read essays, you see, as coded sexual invitations. When they wrote of forests representing wickedness and desire, this was really an indication of delight in the possibility of wickedness and desire with him. He really thought they were all personally addressed to him. He would carry phrases around with him for days, reading them over and over again, to fuel his hysterical libido.'

Perhaps I'm a prude, but the thought of someone masturbating over the contents of a student's essay disgusted me. I wondered why she was telling me all this. Was she testing me or teasing me?

'He was a sick man. I know because I was married to him for almost two years. I'm not now, thank God.'

She paused for moment. Was any of this relevant to Rebecca Morney?

'As I said, it can be difficult for female students. Male lecturers have power. Power can be attractive. Power can be abused. And *is* abused. Unfortunately,' she paused in mid-sentence, 'there are always female students willing to succumb to male power.

And there are always those male members of staff who are more than willing to abuse their power.'

'Do you have someone in mind?'

'These men are everywhere. I'm not naming names. But if you are a good detective, Mr. Renfield, you'll soon know the name or names of the person or persons to whom I refer.'

'You have more than one person in mind?'

'As I said, and I meant it, I'm not naming names.' She stressed the plurality. 'What I will say is this, where there is power, as Michel Foucault contends, there is always resistance. What you are investigating, Mr. Renfield, may well turn out to be an act of resistance.'

She paused as if considering this for a moment, then continued. 'Your best course of action would be to talk to Rebecca's friends.' She paused again, then added as if to clarify the point: 'Talk to other students, Mr. Renfield.'

The sentence was articulated with a definite sense of finality. Her tone of voice was announcing the end of the interview. It didn't bother me, as I had little more that I could usefully ask. I rose from my chair and thanked her for her time.

'May I talk with you again, Dr Smith?' I said in a routine sort of way.

'Of course.' Adding, 'If necessary. You know where to find me. Good day, Mr. Renfield.'

As I stood to leave, she stood also. Stepping from behind her desk, she smiled and then looked rather gloomy as she spoke. 'There is one thing I will tell you that might help. Rebecca told me she was HIV Positive. Actually, she told me she had AIDS. I told her all the usual stuff. You can't catch it from kissing or cuddling, or coughs and sneezes, sharing toilet facilities. You know, that sort of thing.'

I nodded.

'I then detailed the real culprits: sexual intercourse, infected needles, and contaminated blood products. She listened patiently and then simply repeated the claim that she had AIDS.'

Dr Ester Smith removed a pencil from a desk drawer. She held it in her right hand and tapped it gently against the palm of her left hand.

'I made it clear to her that being infected with HIV is not the same as having AIDS. But I also told her that, unfortunately, the latter usually followed the former. However, whether it does or not, one might remain perfectly healthy for several years between HIV and AIDS. Again, she listened patiently and then informed me that everything I had said had already been said by a doctor at St Mary's. She also told me she had been counselled at the hospital.'

I remained silent, waiting.

'Then, as if to soften what she had told me, to remove herself from the pain of it all, she told me that the first authenticated AIDS case in the West had occurred here in Manchester in 1959. She said the man's name was David Carr. It was as if amid the awfulness of it all she just couldn't help being a student. I wanted to laugh, but I knew she would not understand.'

Although I was interested in Manchester's significant role in the history of AIDS, I was determined to remain focused on Rebecca Morney's disappearance. 'Did she say how *she* had contracted the disease?'

'No.'

'Did she mention any names?'

'She told me only that she had AIDS.'

I waited, now certain that Dr Ester Smith was not telling me the whole truth. The silence became overwhelming.

She spoke slowly and deliberately. 'She said she'd contracted AIDS from a member of staff.'

'Someone here at the university?'

'Yes.'

'Who? Did she say who it was?'

'She wouldn't say.'

'Did you ask?'

'Yes, of course I asked,' she replied rather angrily. 'She wouldn't say.'

'Did she say why she was telling you all this?'

'No. But I am her personal tutor.'

I left Dr Ester Smith's office wondering how this information might help my inquiries. Who was the member of staff? Warner? Fish? Trelawny? Someone else? Would knowing help me find Rebecca Morney? Perhaps it was simple: she was in hospital somewhere. I would make the usual inquiries. Finding a missing person in a hospital would be an easy resolution to the case. There was hope in my step as I walked quickly away from the university.

As I crossed All Saints Park, I realised I hadn't asked her for the names of Rebecca Morney's friends. I hesitated, thinking I should return. But it could wait. I had other things to investigate.

Chapter Four

Wednesday.

A light drizzle was beginning to fall outside the window of the offices of the AndTom Detective Agency.

My hospital inquiries had drawn a blank. If Rebecca Morney was in hospital, she was in under an assumed name, or the hospital was not in the Greater Manchester area. I would have to broaden my search. Andi might be able to help.

I was at my desk reading *The Guardian*. Nelson Mandela's victory at the polls was the top story. South Africa was changing at last. I then read, with a different kind of pleasure and satisfaction, the report of United's two-nil victory over Leeds at Elland Road. The result put United two points clear, with a game in hand over nearest rivals Blackburn Rovers.

It was late afternoon when Bill Warner arrived. Andi met him at the door as she was leaving to work on a routine surveillance case. She noticed straightaway that he had been drinking. She directed him to a chair in the hallway and offered him a coffee, which he declined.

'There's someone to see you, Tom. He looks drunk, miserably drunk. He does not look like a happy man. I can smell a confession brewing,' she said, laughing quietly.

I opened the door and addressed Warner: 'I'll be with you in a moment, Dr Warner. Can I get you a coffee?'

He thanked me but said no again. His voice was unsteady. He was trying very hard to control the influence of the alcohol but with little success. He was caught somewhere between what Fish would call precision and indeterminacy. He certainly had no control over the smell of beer that wafted towards me with each word that he spoke. He might have bought mints, I thought. I closed the door and noticed a growing look of excitement on Andi's face.

'Warner! This might be the easy breakthrough, Tom. Do you want me to stay? I'm serious.'

'No. I think I can handle Warner. See you about seven in *The Gardeners Arms*. I'll tell you then if there has been a breakthrough.'

She smiled, nodded, and left.

'Please, do come through, Dr Warner.'

'I have come to talk about Rebecca Morney. I haven't got much time, so I'll get straight to the point.'

He then stopped and looked around a little uncertainly.

I offered him a chair. He sat down. He opened his mouth and words came out. His words were a little slurred. All the while he was staring at the wall behind my head.

'There's not much to tell you. I had an affair with her. Rebecca Morney, I mean. We slept together. Are you shocked? I am. I feel soiled. It's as if I have been untrue to an essential part of my being. I have betrayed something within myself.'

He slumped back in his chair. He was obviously very drunk. There would be little need for questions. If I waited, he would tell me everything. This was going to be very easy.

'After we'd slept together, she asked if I was HIV Positive. I was shocked. I mean, what kind of question is that? Even with today's students that is an awful question, a shocking question.'

I pushed out my lips and tried to look sympathetic. The hospital inquiries may have drawn a blank, but Warner's story would surely take me where I needed to go.

He repeated himself: 'After we'd slept together, she asked if I was HIV Positive. I was shocked, really shocked. I mean, what kind of question is that? Of course, I said no. I mean, what kind of question is that? She seemed disappointed. Can you understand that? Can you even believe it? I would not expect that of even today's students. Really shocking. Disgusting. The nineties are going to be worse than the sixties. Instead of tragedy followed by farce, it is tragedy after tragedy. What are we doing?'

I continued to practice my sympathetic look and tried hard not to seem impatient. I sat in silence and waited.

'I said no, of course. What else could I say? I continued to say no, but she kept on about it for the rest of the evening. It was nothing to be ashamed of, she whined. I must admit that I am HIV Positive, she demanded. The truth didn't seem to matter to her. I had to admit that I was HIV Positive. Well, anyway, I held my ground. I stuck to the truth. I wasn't HIV Positive. I told her to stop asking me stupid questions and expecting even more stupid answers. I was finding it hard not to become very angry with her.'

I was thinking about what Dr Ester Smith had told me, so I had to ask. 'What made you so sure?' It seemed a rather impertinent question. I regretted asking it. I retreated into a memory of Warner's books. I suddenly wondered why I'd had to study *Shirley* instead of *Jane Eyre* or *Wuthering Heights*. It was the same with Thomas Hardy. *Under The Greenwood Tree* instead of *The Return of the Native* or *Jude the Obscure*. We always had to study the less well-known books. Why?

I looked at Warner. He was not offended. He was suddenly very open in his manner, almost sober, but not quite.

'As a matter of fact, before the affair I had been celibate for almost two years. God knows why.'

He caught my expression. 'No, I mean it literally. I was celibate for spiritual reasons. It was a religious thing.'

He laughed a little self-consciously. 'Deny the flesh and all that. Now I'll probably be punished for my little lapse.' He was serious again. For a moment he was lost in thought. Probably worrying about the weight of his lapse. But he seemed to be winning his struggle against the effects of the beer.

I asked the obvious question. 'Being celibate for almost two years does not guarantee that you are not HIV Positive. So, what makes you so certain?'

He thought about it for a moment. Experience warned me to expect deception. The seemingly obvious is often a trap.

'Dr Warner, you cannot be certain,' I prompted.

'I can. I am certain. As I said, I was celibate until my affair with Rebecca Morney.'

I was becoming a little tired. I had no wish to sit through a drunken discourse on the sins of the flesh. Warner's presence lowered my boredom threshold. He'd had the same effect on me as a student. People who think they mean well are not always the best at being engagingly meaningful.

I prompted again. 'But you know as well as I do that-'

He interrupted. 'Look, I know I wasn't HIV Positive before my affair with Rebecca Morney because, as I said, I had been celibate for almost two years and my celibacy had begun with a negative AIDS test.'

He rose from his chair and walked to the window. 'Do you mind if I open it?'

'No, go ahead.'

My boredom was draining away fast. Why had he taken an AIDS test? Should I have asked or waited for him to tell me?

He stood silent and still with his head out of the window. I remained seated and waited. The rain was falling harder. It gave the impression of bars outside the window. For a moment I felt like a prisoner, trapped inside with Warner and his dirty little secrets. After a few minutes, he straightened his body and turned to face me. His hair and face were wet. Very wet. He used a pale green handkerchief to dry his face. He then blew his nose. He no longer looked drunk, just tired and unhappy. He adjusted his dickie-bow and returned to his seat.

'You are wondering why I had an AIDS test? I had the test

after I had separated from my wife. That is the explanation. It has nothing to do with the disappearance of Rebecca Morney.'

It became obvious that he wasn't going to say much more about it. He was probably right, his relationship with his wife had no bearing on my search for Rebecca Morney. I changed the subject. 'When did you last see her? Rebecca Morney, I mean,' I added, a little unnecessarily.

He nodded. His expression grew sullen.

'I'm not sure. About a month ago, I think. Maybe five weeks. I only saw her the once. I mean. Well, you know what I mean.'

I nodded my head quickly. I didn't want the details, but I was curious.

I thought of the photograph in my inside pocket. I thought about Rebecca Morney's beautiful and compelling eyes. Why would she want a relationship with Warner? And then that other question, who was behind the camera? Was it Warner? Had she really left it by mistake in Fish's office? It was all becoming a little sordid, but also a little more interesting.

Warner was deep in thought again, as if puzzling over some detail of literary scholarship. I should have asked him about the photograph. But before I could, he started to lecture me again.

'My greatest lapse wasn't the sex. That was of very short duration, a moment of sin in a sea of temptation. I cannot be blamed much for that. My greatest lapse was playing false with the truth. I eventually told her the lie that she so wanted to be true. I told her the stupid rumours were true. I told her I was HIV Positive. In fact, I told her I was more than HIV Positive, I told her I had full-blown AIDS. I just wanted to hurt her, frighten her with her own frail mortality. But she just laughed. It was a sickening laugh, full of triumph and certainty. I will never forget her laughter; it was absolutely shocking. It was a horrid display of humanity devoid of all goodness. I am thankful it hasn't yet entered my dreams. Luckily, I have my faith.'

His face formed a puzzled expression.

'Why she wanted it to be true, I cannot for the life of me understand.'

'Did you ask her?'

'No. I was too disgusted, too shocked with the question and her sickening laughter. I was even more disgusted and shocked with my own answer. Answering her question, in the way she wanted it answered, allowed me to leave. I had no interest in her or her reasons. Our transaction had been purely physical. Something to regret, but nothing more. I said I had AIDS and then I left. I had to leave quickly to stop her laughter from devastating my soul.'

I wanted to produce my own laughter at the self-pitying melodrama of it all. Instead, I asked him the obvious question. 'Do you know where Rebecca Morney is now?'

'I do not know, and I do not care, I really mean it, I do not bloody care. I don't normally swear, but this is a language she would understand. It is a language she shares with many other students. So disappointing.'

He was silent for a moment. 'I've been writing a book - a very moral book - on literary criticism. It has grown from my incomprehension at the cultural tastes - I use the phrase loosely - of my students.'

He was frantically waving his fingers around making gestures to indicate inverted commas.

'I doubt I'll ever finish it now. I'll miss its completion, but I won't miss Rebecca Morney,' he said with a self-absorbed pomposity that his heavy consumption of beer only worked to amplify.

The finality seemed a little forced. How hurt was Warner? What had she hurt? His heart? His pride? His book? His soul? Was he involved in Rebecca Morney's disappearance? Was he dangerous?

'Did you ever take a photograph of Rebecca?' I asked, hopefully.

He ignored my question. 'She wanted me to be HIV Positive. She took a sick delight in the possibility. 'Now I'm HIV Positive,' she said. 'You've infected me.' She smiled as she said it, a crooked, evil smile. Of course, I knew I hadn't, but her attitude so disgusted and shocked me, I let her think I had. I left her believing she was certain to be HIV Positive. I left her with this death sentence. For a small, shocking moment I really wanted it to be true.'

If Warner was not the source of Rebecca Morney's infection, who was? She had told Dr Ester Smith that she had been told, quite categorically, by St Mary's that she had AIDS. Either Warner was not telling the truth or Rebecca Morney had been infected by someone else. Again, I wondered if knowing would help me find her.

'Honestly, I have no idea where she is. I didn't even know she was missing. Before you told me, I had no idea.'

'She's been missing for almost a week.'

'How can you tell? How can you be so sure? You were a student. You know what it's like.'

'She's not been seen for almost a week. Friends are getting worried.'

I looked out of the window. 'It looks like the rain is stopping,' I said.

He turned towards the window and nodded.

'Do you know where Rebecca Morney is hiding?' He looked confused. 'As I said, I've been hired to find her. Do you have any idea where she might be?'

'No. Have you tried her friends? She had a particular friend. Let me think.' Warner's thought processes rumbled to a halt. 'Sally Wilson,' he exclaimed.

He reached into his briefcase to locate an address. He copied an address from a little green book and handed it to me.

'I shouldn't really do this. But good luck.'

'Thanks,' I said, wondering why Warner had a student's address in his address book. Another shocking moral lapse?

We shook hands and he started to leave. I had to ask the question again. 'Did you take photographs of Rebecca Morney?'

'Photographs? Photographs? Photographs? What do you mean?' His face became more distorted each time he repeated the word.

'Do I look like the sort of man who would take photos of students?'

I rephrased the question. 'Did you ever take a photograph of Rebecca Morney?'

'No, certainly not. What kind of person do you think I am?'

I reached into the draw and pulled out the photograph Fish had given me. I handed it to Warner. At first, he looked relieved. He had obviously thought I meant a different kind of photograph. Relief quickly gave way to something like horror. He held the photograph as if it might suddenly explode.

'I did not take this photograph. I did not take any photographs of Rebecca Morney.'

He hurried out before I could say much more. To be truthful, I was glad to see the back of him. I decided that I would only interview him again if I really needed to know more details. Warner was a pathetic case. He'd probably go home now with an expensive bottle of wine, and cry himself to sleep, while quoting poetic banalities from those dreadful nineteenth-century hymns I remembered him loving so much.

Alone in the office, I paced up and down. I was even more puzzled than before. How could there be a rumour that Warner had AIDS? Why did she run the risk of catching AIDS? Why did she invite the risk? It didn't seem to make sense. I remembered Fish's words, repeated in seminar after seminar, 'something that doesn't make much sense may be the only clue we have to what is really significant.'

The rain had finally stopped. There seemed even the possibility of sunshine. The wind had picked up a little. It wafted in through the window Warner had left open. I walked over quickly and closed it. The street was surprisingly empty. I was briefly overcome with a feeling of deja vu.

I was about to leave when the phone rang.

'Hello. My name's Sally Wilson. I'm a friend of Rebecca Morney's. Dr Warner asked me to give you a call about Rebecca.'

He had already told her. In some ways this came as more of a surprise than the story he had told me about Rebecca Morney's desire for AIDS. Warner was more complicated than I thought.

'Oh. Hi. Thank you for calling. Would it be possible for us to meet for a chat?'

'Yes, of course. But I don't know where she is.'

'I would still like to have a chat, if that's okay?'

'Yes, of course. Where should we meet?'

'If it's okay with you, I would prefer it if we could meet where you live.'

She didn't hesitate. 'Okay.' She then gave me the address. 'Would around 4.30 tomorrow be okay?'

I said yes and thanked her. I put the phone down and opened the window. I sat there for a long time looking out and wondering how helpful Sally Wilson might be.

That night I fell asleep remembering everything she'd said.

Chapter Five

Thursday.

Fish had left a message on the answer machine. He wanted to discuss progress. He said he would call at the AndTom office on Friday at noon unless I made contact and indicated otherwise.

I left my apartment at 11.40. I was greeted by a beautiful sunny morning. The warm stillness pressed against me, wanting me to know that summer was on its way. Two black birds crossed the otherwise empty sky behind the new student accommodation. I watch them circle and then disappear. I looked for their return, but they had gone.

I always walked the same route to the AndTom offices. Through the subway and across the roundabout beneath the Mancunian Way and into Cambridge Street, passed the new student halls of residence; passed the chimneys and warehouses of nineteenth-century Manchester; passed the squatters behind the broken windows of the old Dunlop factory; passed the glorified soup kitchen that is the Jerusalem Cafe; passed the Hotspur House, the home of the Hotspur Press.

Walking under the railway bridge and left into Whitworth Street, I entered a different kind of Manchester. Here are the green shoots of renaissance. Beneath the railway arches of the Manchester to Liverpool line, the oldest commercial railway in the world, there were wine bars, cafes, and restaurants. These were not places for the patrons of the Jerusalem Cafe. I'm not even sure if they were intended for me. I had yet to discover if

I would feel welcomed.

I crossed the street and passed the 24-Hour Snooker Hall and the newly established Canal Bar. I turned right into Albion Street, passed The Hacienda, then across the Rochdale Canal and between, on the left, the G. Mex Centre and, on the right, the Cheerleaders American Bar. At the Briton's Protection, where it is said Henry Hunt delivered his address before the drunken butchery of Peterloo, I turned right into Great Bridgewater Street. The AndTom Detective Agency was situated where the street curved left, back toward the centre of the city.

I was in the office by 11.53. I picked up the mail, checked the answering machine and made myself a Darjeeling tea. I removed the photograph of Rebecca Morney from the brown envelope in which Fish had placed it. I looked at her beautiful dark eyes and said, 'What am I missing?' I stared at her face, and I wondered if this was really Rebecca Morney. She looked different since my conversation with Warner, but I was trying hard not to judge her.

Fish arrived at 11.58. He was carrying a large green box.

'I thought you might be able to use these,' he said, handing me the box. It was heavier than I had imagined. I had to tighten my grip. I looked at the box. It contained twenty-four bottles of Chinese beer. I had never had Chinese beer before. I wondered if he had noticed our fridge full of beer from around the world. Probably not, I thought. But this would make an admirable addition to the collection. I looked at Fish and smiled and said thank you. He then began to tell me about his trip around the Tsingtao Brewery. 'We were taken around the brewery by a guide who spoke English at a hundred miles an hour. I think she was intimidated when she heard my friend speak English. All I really understood was that the brewery had been German until the revolution. But the beer is good. I'm sure you will like it.'

I thanked him again.

'Don't worry,' he said, 'I didn't carry these all the way from

China, I bought them today in Chinatown.'

I put the beer down behind my desk.

'How are things, Tom? I believe you attended Ester's lecture on detective fiction. What did you think? Did you learn anything? Pick up any new tricks? She's very good, you know,' he added in a rather patronising manner.

Fish folded his arms and settled down to one of his favourite topics, rubbishing the work of a colleague. He would often shock students by the way he talked about other members of academic staff. Sometimes he discussed the inadequacies of their teaching, at other times he mocked the pretensions of their research. But he was most entertaining when he talked about them just as people. He would pretend not to notice that his audience was both surprized and amused.

'The problem with psychoanalysis is its assumption that causes are always ultimately rooted in ahistorical processes. Ester's account of detective fiction is itself a fiction. To understand the emergence of the genre we must pay attention to history.

'Psychoanalysis and detective fiction were both born in the same historical moment. Like psychoanalysis, detective fiction seeks to discover the truth by making patterns where other people see only an arbitrary and random selection of details.

He was in full flow now, enjoying himself. The fact that he was sitting in my office, paying me £60 a day, plus expenses, to find a lost student, seemed of little importance to him. He continued as if he were addressing a big international conference in somewhere like Barcelona or Beijing. He was now on his feet, arms gesturing towards the window and beyond.

'Clues and symptoms are analysed in much the same way. Both detective and analyst are confronted by an arrangement of details from which they must make sense. The scene must be deconstructed to make stand out the significant detail or details. Sometimes the detail is significant by its absence. Take the famous example when Inspector Gregory asks Sherlock

Holmes if there is anything he should take note of, and Holmes replies, 'The curious incident of the dog in the night-time.' Gregory responds that the dog did nothing. To which Holmes sagely replies, 'That was the curious incident."

I wanted to interrupt the lecture. But I knew from bitter experience that interrupting Fish was never a good idea. I tried to relax and pretend I was in Barcelona or Beijing. I have been to Barcelona, so I imagined Beijing. Perhaps Shanghai would be better? My mind was beginning to wander. I was finding it more and more difficult to concentrate on Fish's critique of Dr Ester Smith's lecture. But the words continued.

'This is all okay as far as it goes. The trouble is, it doesn't go far enough. The detective makes the complexity of the city readable. He fulfils the bourgeois desire to simplify the city and the activities of its inhabitants. The private eye is really the panoptic eye long dreamed of by power.

'The detective is a bourgeois invention; the men who made the cities, and made the cities strange and dangerous, bringing together into an apparently amorphous mass, people from the countryside and beyond, they made the detective. The detective is a fantasy, a dream figure who promises to decode the increasing and very threatening anonymity of the city. Sherlock Holmes, for example, embodies both the reckless desires of the bourgeoisie to penetrate the dark and disturbing urban body, and the growing anxiety that the city is a language out of control, a language spoken without understanding. They speak the language like they know what it means. But they haven't a clue.'

He smiled, overly contented.

'In short, the detective promises to read the city. But it is a fantasy, of course. A reassuring vision which existed nowhere else but in the fantasy of detective fiction.

'True, the nineteenth century saw the introduction of real detectives. But they only disturbed the bourgeoisie's sense of the freedom of the individual threatened by an encroaching state. It was only in fiction that the reassurance of a detective could be found.'

I was beginning to wonder if Fish was leading up to making a point. It was all very interesting. And yes, he might have valid points to raise against Dr Ester Smith's famous lecture on Lacan and detective fiction, but we were supposedly here to find a lost student. Then again, being paid to listen to a lecture was a novel experience.

'Anyway, that's enough academic talk.'

He spoke the word academic in a way I would never have expected from him. It was as if he had suddenly discovered that such knowledge was of little significance to the real demands of life. Was it that what defined him suddenly no longer seemed so solid?

Then his tone changed. Once again, he seemed larger than life. 'What progress, Tom? What progress have *you* made? Do you know where Rebecca Morney is hiding?'

I opened a black notebook and quickly assessed my notes. 'You were right about Bill Warner. He did have an affair with Rebecca Morney.'

I thought I detected a brief smile move quickly across his face. Its fleeting presence was quickly replaced by an expression of dark bitterness, which just as quickly faded into a strange look of brutal triumph and then quiet satisfaction.

I continued, 'Warner denied it at our first meeting. But he came to see me later to confess what he described as his 'guilt.''

'Typical. That's so typical of Warner. Delay followed by melodrama.'

Fish grinned triumphantly. Confusion was banished. His emotions now seemed under control. He had been right, and he was very pleased with himself. Here was the satisfaction of knowing once again that one is always right.

Then in a mocking tone, he began to quiz me. 'Did he cry? Did he breakdown and cry like a baby? Did he say how sorry he was? Did he mumble inanities about God and the soul? Or did he quote some awful sentiment from one of those silly nineteenth-century novels he loves so much? Perhaps he cited something from those truly dreadful hymns he's forever quoting? The poor man at the gate,' he said, laughing. 'That kind of unbelievable nonsense.'

These were all rhetorical questions. There was no need for me to respond. I was required only to watch and listen as Fish enjoyed himself.

'Did he go into details?'

Fish was controlled again. In fact, Fish was in control again.

'Only to say that the affair was brief.'

'I bet it was.'

Fish was laughing like a schoolboy. He was rocking his chair on its back legs and laughing out loud. It was a deep belly laugh that reverberated throughout his whole shaking body. It was the kind of laughter that made me think I should close the window. He was a public-school boy again.

'I bet it was. Very, very brief.'

He was now laughing so much that I thought he might fall from his chair. But his laughter was very infectious. I had to try very hard not to start laughing myself. In a different context I would have just let go. But here in my office, it just did not seem appropriate. I suppose it seemed unprofessional.

The rocking and the laughter gradually stopped. There were a few moments of silence and stillness. Then he slowly gathered himself and spoke with a new seriousness.

'What could she have possibly seen in Warner? You've seen her photograph, Tom. You're a detective, tell me, if you can, what could a woman like Rebecca - Rebecca Morney,' he corrected himself - 'see in a man like Warner?'

I shrugged my shoulders and remained silent. It wasn't just a question of her being very attractive and Warner being unattractive. These things are always relative and conditional on circumstances. But I could not envisage, no matter how hard I tried, any circumstances in which she would want to sleep with him. I remembered what he had said about AIDS, but it just did not make sense. The more I considered it, the less sense it made.

'Did he mention his *book*? He must have done. He tells everyone he meets about his *book*. Why he was given a sabbatical to write a book about what he doesn't understand, I'll never know. Perhaps it was the *book* with Rebecca Morney? It masked his profound unattractiveness. No, not even the promise of that awful book could have attracted her. Surely not.'

Fish was laughing again. He stopped suddenly and quickly composed himself. 'Is that all he said, he had an affair? Is that all?'

The sudden change of tone and topic was a little disturbing. I tried hard to pretend not to have noticed. I simply answered, yes.

Why was I holding back all the stuff about AIDS? I couldn't quite explain to myself why I wasn't being frank with Fish. After all, Fish was my client. Fish was paying me to gather all relevant information. I tried to convince myself that this wasn't relevant information. But I couldn't. Maybe I would tell Fish the details when I had a fuller picture of all the relevant events, but not just yet. Not just now.

'What happens now?'

'I continue to look for Rebecca Morney?'

I looked hard at Fish, and then I asked him, 'That's still what you want me to do? Right?'

'Yes. Of course.'

Fish tapped his fingers on the table and then said in a rather forced confidential tone, 'I've found a way to get the money to pay for all this from the university.' Fish announced this as if it justified the continuation of the investigation.

There was a moment of awkward silence. Fish broke it with a confident smile and a question. 'What's your next move, Tom, further investigate Warner, see how deep in it he is? Discover if he knows where she is?'

'No,' I said slowly, trying not to appear rude. 'I'm confident that Warner does not know Rebecca Morney's whereabouts. Whether she has disappeared or is in hiding somewhere, I am confident that Warner does not know where she is.'

'Are you sure?' He sounded very disappointed.

'Yes. I'm very sure.'

'How can you be so sure?'

'He could of course be a great actor, but everything he told me and showed me indicated that he did not know.'

Announcing it in this way made him appear less confident. I was sure that the relationship between Warner and Rebecca Morney was history in every sense. But to be on the safe side, I wouldn't close entirely my interest in him. Not just yet. However, I didn't feel any compunction to inform Fish of these considerations. Again, I wasn't sure why I was keeping things from a client.

'As soon as you locate her, you will let me know. I mean the minute you locate her. You understand?'

I nodded and forced a brief smile. 'The minute I find her, she's yours.'

'This is very important to me, Tom.'

'I know. As soon as I find her, you will know immediately.'

He smiled, a new confidence spreading across his face. We shook hands and he left. He just disappeared. He was here and then he was gone.

His laughter, however, echoed down the stairwell and out on to the streets of Manchester. They say laughter is infectious. I wondered about the nature of the disease carried in Fish's sardonic chuckles. What did I have to do to remain immune? The sooner I found Rebecca Morney, the better it might be for my health.

Chapter Six

Thursday.

Late afternoon. The sun was still shining. It was a sparkling afternoon. It was the kind of springtime that poets sing about. Life suddenly seemed more intense. I felt more alive than I had done in ages. I removed my dark glasses and rubbed my nose. Life is good, I thought. I was almost singing as I lifted my hand to knock on the heavy wooden door.

Sally Wilson had told me to arrive about four-thirty. She was supposedly Rebecca Morney's best friend. I was hoping she would have some idea of her whereabouts. When she'd phoned, she'd said she didn't know where her friend was, but I was hoping that would change when we were face to face. It did seem she wanted to help. But that might just be curiosity. Or worse still, she might intend to mislead. Being too helpful can be a warning sign. You wonder who they are really trying to help, if help at all. If Rebecca Morney did not want to be found, a best friend might not be the best person to ask. But now Sally Wilson was the only person I thought might know.

I stood in the doorway and looked around at the other houses. The house was Edwardian. What had once been the home of a prosperous bourgeois family, was now the playground for a revolving group of students. The difference may have horrified the original owners. It would certainly have surprised them. What had once been a very desirable residential area, was now just a short distance from the area of Manchester the tabloids had started to call names like 'Baby Beirut' and 'Britain's Bronx.' According to local media, drive-by drug killings were becoming almost commonplace. Never the real villains, almost always the young couriers: bicycle wheels spinning in the road in the last rites of a wasted life.

It was a shared house. I was a little disappointed. I had been hoping against hope that she would have a flat of her own within the house. I wanted to be alone with her. That way there was more chance of getting close to the truth. An audience would only increase the chances of misunderstanding. It would also increase the chances of a performance. The little private things that are so important would not be spoken, or at least not spoken about clearly.

I knocked again on the heavy wooden door and waited.

'Hi. You must be Tom Renfield. I'm Sally Wilson. Please, do come in.'

She was dressed in blue Wrangler jeans and a yellow and green, striped cotton shirt. Her feet were bare. She was tall with shoulder length dark brown hair. As she lifted her hand to welcome me, her breasts moved beneath her shirt.

Sally was very friendly and welcoming; more friendly and welcoming than I had a right to expect. Perhaps she really did intend to be helpful? Or perhaps this was a warning? I would have to be on my guard. I had to be very careful.

She showed me in to a large, badly furnished room, which exuded an odour of stale food, alcohol, and the sweet smell of dope. Most of the furniture looked as if it had seen better days. In the centre of the room was a large wooden table littered with empty cans, half-filled coffee cups, magazines, newspapers, CDs, and books.

There were two other people in the room, a woman and a man. He was tall with long black hair. He was wearing jeans and an orange t-shirt. Like Sally, he was barefooted. The woman had on a short denim skirt and a white cotton shirt. She was wearing a pair of purple trainers.

The woman looked relaxed. The man looked tense. He looked at me for a moment and then seemed reassured by what he saw. I don't know what he'd expected.

The man went to a cupboard drawer and removed a small wooden box. The box was very dark red. On its lid I could see faded characters that looked Chinese. From the wooden box he removed some cigarette papers, some rolling tobacco, and a block of cannabis resin. He proceeded to skin up. The two women smiled helplessly, as if at the behaviour of a spoilt child. He smiled in response. Then he turned to me, smiling. I could tell that this wasn't going to be the first time he had rolled up today.

'Solved any interesting cases recently?' he said, slightly aggressively. There was a hint of a slur in his voice.

'Ignore Guy. He's a bore,' said the black woman. She spoke without looking up from her book. I couldn't read the title, but it looked like a book of poetry. She introduced herself as Polly. This time she put her book down and got to her feet.

We shook hands. 'You must hear that all the time?' she said.

'Not really,' I replied, trying to sound cool.

Polly laughed. She was easily impressed. I looked at her bright purple trainers.

'They're great, aren't they? I bought them yesterday at the market in Ashton. Louise told me about it. Have you ever been? It's great. You should go.'

As I wondered who Louise might be, I told Polly I had been, but that it was a long time ago. I also told her that her trainers were indeed great. She smiled a long-satisfied smile.

Guy continued to roll a joint. He was working carefully on an old school desk. On the wall above the desk was a very large poster, bright yellow letters on a spring green background. The words said: ***You Can Do All Kinds Of Things If You Need To Enough***. It looked less impressive close up. The paint had not been evenly applied. Next to it was another poster - also homemade - **It's Never Too Late To Have A Happy Childhood.** Both looked like the work of a talented child. I immediately recognized the style. The poster I had seen in Dr Ester Smith's office was obviously the work of the same artist.

Guy noticed my interest. He lit the completed joint, inhaled deeply, and began a brief explanation of the posters. 'They are both Rebecca's. This one,' he said pointing to the yellow letters on a spring green background, 'is a quotation from some stupid children's book, *Geraldine and the Pig*, I think it's called. The other's something she heard at a party back home in richland.'

'You mean she painted them?,' I asked.

He mumbled something, laughing.

'It's *Gertrude and the Frog*,' said Sally, matter-of-factly. Turning to me, smiling, she said, 'It was Rebecca's favourite book as a child.'

She said something to Guy, and then she turned to me, 'Yes, she painted them. I like them very much. Do you like them?'

She said the last sentence with a sparkle in her eyes. She stood waiting for my response with her legs apart and her arms behind her back. She caught me a little off balance. I coughed and said, 'Yes, I like them very much.' I was unsure whether this was a joke or not. I tried to look serious, while continuing to smile. Should I ask about the poster in Dr Ester Smith's office?

Guy seemed oblivious to Sally's intervention or my uncertainty. Inhaling deeply every two or three sentences, he explained the origins of the posters. 'She was supposed to be giving them to a long-forgotten admirer, a muscle-bound friend from back home in richland: some athletic, bourgeois twat. He came to visit at the end of the first semester. Not a success. He hates students.'

'He certainly hated you,' said Polly.

'Just jealous, that's all.'

'Yeah, right,' said Polly and Sally in almost perfect unison. They both laughed. Then Guy laughed. His laughter began as irony but quickly became the real thing. The dope was taking more and more control.

I knew that Sally was looking at me without obviously looking. I could feel her scrutiny and I liked it. I looked at her more openly. She caught my gaze, like a small child might grab hold of a flying tennis ball. We smiled at each other: secret smiles, capable of making promises. As if to break the spell, she asked me if I would like a drink. I responded that I would love a cup of tea. Before she left the room, she took a deep drag on Guy's joint. My eyes followed her out. She returned with a pot of Darjeeling tea. It was as if she knew. I thanked her as she filled up my cup.

Polly helped herself to tea and then said: 'I saw you in Ester Smith's lecture on Wednesday. What did you think of her theory of detective *fiction*, you being a detective and all?'

'It isn't her theory, dummy. It's Jacques Lacan's,' said Guy.

'No, it isn't dummy,' said Sally, coming to Polly's rescue. 'It's Ester's theory of how Lacanian theory might be used to explore and explain detective fiction. Lacan does not write about detective fiction.'

'He doesn't write about anything because he's dead, dummy.' He followed this by uncontrollable laughter. When he laughed, he seemed to lose about ten years. A little boy lost in the euphoric ebb and flow of the dope.

Ignoring Guy's laughter, Sally's defence gave Polly the confidence to continue her questioning of me. 'What did you think? Is it really like that?'

Guy was stumbling back with a vengeance: 'Regardless of whose theory it is, she was talking about detective fiction. Fiction, Polly. you know, there is fact and there is fiction. Sherlock Holmes is fiction. Tom Renfield here is fact. Well, I think he's fact. To be fair, we haven't gathered all the evidence yet,' he chuckled, louder and louder.

I answered Polly politely, 'It's not as interesting as in theory, fact or fiction.'

'Anyway,' said Guy rather pompously, 'she should be talking about science fiction. Detective fiction is so modernist. The postmodern genre is science fiction.'

Guy seemed to talk forever about modernism and postmodernism. Sometimes his argument stumbled towards a conclusion, but mostly he rambled from point to point. It was a great relief when Sally changed the topic of conversation. She spoke loudly, clearly intending to shut up Guy.

'Tom wants to know things about Rebecca?'

'Don't we all,' said Guy, laughing to himself. 'Sally, you've already told us all that,' he continued, rather mockingly. 'Remember, you briefed us thoroughly just before the detective arrived.'

Sally looked at Guy. She was a little embarrassed. She was also a little angry. Her anger was that of an indulgent older sister to a naughty younger brother, but she wanted him to be quiet.

Polly came to her rescue. 'Well, let's talk to Tom about Rebecca,' she said. 'We are all sick of listening to your dopey ramblings about science fiction and postmodernism. Tom wants to know things about Rebecca. He wants to know where she is. We all do.'

'Spending money is the answer to that question. That's what she likes doing. And that's what she does best. It's her only real interest. It's the only thing she is really any good at. She once lost her purse containing one of her credit cards. The person who found it phoned her and claimed to be from the bank. He asked her to confirm certain details, including her pin number. She gave him the pin number without a second thought. He hung up immediately and started spending her money. When it was pointed out to her how stupid she had been, she wasn't even bothered. It was only money, she said. With an endless supply, she wasn't too worried about losing some. After all, Daddy had plenty more to give her.'

'You don't like her, do you?' I asked Guy, casually.

'She's okay, I suppose. I just resent her capitalist mentality. She's just so materialistic. She thinks she must have everything.

Must own everything. The way she sees the world is in terms of things she can afford and things she can't afford *yet*. The whole purpose of life is to gradually limit the items in the second category. Nirvana is achieved when the second category disappears altogether. It's a wonderful view of life's purpose. She's consumer capitalism's dream subject.'

'Oh, come on, Guy,' said Polly crossly. 'You're just bitter. You'd like more of what she has, and you know it.'

Guy was suddenly very angry, but he controlled himself. He forced a mocking laugh.

Turning to me, Polly continued, 'He'd like more of Rebecca full stop. That's his problem. Rebecca doesn't want anything that Guy's got.'

Guy controlled himself, but the mocking laughter was drying up quickly.

'I know that. I'm too young for Rebecca. I'm not old enough yet to be a lecturer. It's a funny word, *lecturer*, isn't it?'

'What do you mean? Was Rebecca seeing a member of the teaching staff at the university?' I tried to sound casual, but I knew I had jumped in too quickly. I was thinking of Warner and Rebecca Morney. Perhaps it was common knowledge? Fish had no need to worry about passing on information that was confidential.

Guy looked a little irritated. My attempt at casualness had not fooled him. 'I didn't mean anything. I'm just a bit stoned,' he said stubbornly.

My visit was not proving too successful.

'You're the detective - work it out.' Guy's voice now sounded even more irritated.

'Work what out?' I said, wondering why he was so irritated.

He smiled and I smiled. But we were not about to start laughing. Nor were we fooling each other.

I went to the toilet. I had forgotten about the normal state of student toilets. This was something I did not miss. When I returned to the living room, the conversation continued but without revealing much of direct relevance to my search for Rebecca Morney. No one knew, or would admit they knew, where she was hiding.

We drank more tea, Jasmine this time, and then with the usual pleasantries I left, leaving my AndTom card with Sally, after having written my home number on the back. Just in case. But in case of what, I wasn't sure.

I walked back to my car thinking that, as a responsible citizen, I should phone the cops about the dope. But it probably went against the grain of the detective's code of honour. I would have to check what it said about dope smoking.

As I began to consider whether I should question Sally and her friends again, I started to feel a little dizzy. Perhaps it was the result of a couple of hours of passive dope smoking. I decided to go home to lie down for a while. Sleep it off.

Chapter Seven

I parked the car outside my apartment. The day was still warm, so I didn't put my jacket back on. The action of swinging the jacket on to my arm felt different. I felt different. The movement of jacket and arm produced a trace of colour, a wonderful rainbow of colours dancing across the screen of my vision. I moved my other arm through the warm, still air. Another bright rainbow of colours trailed after it. I began to laugh. I didn't know why. I didn't know what I was laughing at. Unlocking the door to the apartment was very difficult. The key wouldn't go in the lock. Eventually, the door opened. But had it taken several minutes, or had it taken much longer? I was finding it very difficult to measure time. What I had always taken for granted, now seemed strange, moving at a new pace in new directions, in new contexts.

I was just closing the door when a taxi arrived. A voice called from the taxi for me to wait. I tried to concentrate on the voice. It was a woman's voice. I knew the voice. I concentrated very hard. The voice belonged to Sally Wilson. She paid the taxi driver and joined me in the doorway. I was laughing again. She looked concerned. She helped me up the stairs and into the apartment.

'Can I stay for a while?' she asked. Her words hovered in the air like birds on the breeze. I waited for their safe landing. She also waited.

I said, 'Yes,' eventually. The word seemed to take a very long time to articulate. It seemed such a big word.

Suddenly I stopped laughing. There was a gap without laughter, and I had to use it to find out what was happening.

She tried to explain what had happened. But it was already too late. I was already far too gone. And then I was laughing again. I was falling away from the ordinary world. I was falling fast, very fast. I was falling into a world of swirling colours and overlapping noises. It felt as if I was being born.

Someone came towards me out of a rainbow blur. It wasn't her, but it was someone. It was a woman. I was falling faster and faster. A woman stared back with graveyard eyes. I looked away, fearful for my sanity.

The music pulled at my stomach. I thought I heard a reassuring voice. But I couldn't be sure. Was I alone? The music moved around me, forming a visible wave of sound. I was the beach upon which it was breaking. The horizon was a dance of bright colours. Suddenly I was on a beach, a horseshoe harbour, green sea, palm trees and a warm sea breeze. Waves of different sounds falling on yellow sand.

I was walking in naked wonder. I heard a woman's voice whispering, *To see a world in a grain of sand and heaven in a wildflower. Hold infinity in the palm of your hand and eternity in an hour.* The words echoed into silence.

The music pulled me back. I was somewhere else. Safe again. She came towards me out of a rainbow blur, tempting me with a handful of coloured dust. I was a man stumbling through the clichés and fictions of a goldmine romance.

The rain poured down in another place, another time. Trees danced wildly in the wind. I heard someone say I was being born again. What was happening? Was this madness? I stumbled forward.

A hand touched my head and the anxiety subsided quietly, draining away into nothingness. I was suddenly overwhelmed with a blissful feeling of oneness with the world. I was crossing the border back in to the Real. She was crossing the border with me. There was no one to ask for our passports.

An explosion of rainbows and then my sense of self was disintegrating fast. The very obviousness of reality was dissolving, fragmenting into a multitude of other realities; a rainbow world of imploding and exploding colours.

Then the sunshine came. I stood by a solitary tree, beneath a rainbow. It was a beautiful garden full of cherry blossom. The perfume held me in a gentle embrace. Whispers played around my ears. I watched the sunlight fade to moonlight. A gentle rain began to fall. Someone held my hand. Happy tears fell from my eyes. A hand caressed my neck. I felt safe again.

But it wasn't over yet. The sky clouded angrily. The gentle rain became a thunderstorm. Lightening crashed. I knew enough not to be beneath a tree. But it was too late. The thunder roared; the lightening cracked. Then there was silence, a visible silence that walked upon the earth, a friendly silence that called my name, a special name known only to silence. I walked hand in hand with silence.

Suddenly in a hallway, I stumbled. Arms reached down to me. I began to walk again, towards a door. The door opened. In the garden were clouds talking in a forbidden language. It was a sad garden. Objects blurred in a wild lysergic sky. It was the moment of birth and time to go to sea.

The waves pounded the planks. The tattered sails flapped to the dance of the breeze. I watched as my senses changed places and combined in a dance beyond understanding. I was breaking up. I wanted to say, 'Who am I?' But the words wouldn't come. There were no more words to come. But I couldn't think of that, it was too disturbing.

Suddenly I thought of a woman alone. Every day she became less herself. Every day she lost a little more. I was overwhelmed by the threat of madness. Gripped by terror, I tried to scream. But there were no more words to come. Dark, disturbing colours emerged from her mouth. Her mouth was a graveyard. Every gravestone was a broken promise. There was only one thought, large and unbearable - her mouth was a graveyard, and it would soon open to consume all within its dark and disturbing madness.

I was slipping. I was slipping into her graveyard mouth.

Arms reached out to embrace me, to stop my fall. They held me as her mouth slipped away.

The face changed. It grew younger. Dark eyes in a pale face, lost in a landscape of frozen traffic. I needed to speak to her. But she was gone. I wanted to follow, but I knew that was impossible.

I was overwhelmed by the sound of waves crashing on a beach. The noise suddenly gave way to the opening drumming on a Beatles' song. It just repeated for a very long time, slowly getting less audible.

Then another woman, smiling warmly. She did not speak, but the bright colours emanating from her mouth softened my terror into anxiety and then into a warm sense of togetherness. Suddenly I could speak the language of the colours.

Her smile dripped softly on my fevered brow. Her body was bliss. She gave me a rainbow. She was helping me rebuild myself. I was slowly becoming whole again.

Suddenly I was overwhelmed by the simplicity of everything. Complexity itself became simple. I was drifting in the rhythm of an all-engulfing music, a rhythm of beautiful repetition. Vibrating on the simple pulse of life, I stood at the shoreline of myself. The sea came in and the sea went out, slowly. The sand was bright yellow, and the sea was very shallow and very green.

I could still use my voice, but I was increasingly aware that it was a very clumsy instrument of communication. There was no need for talking; I was tuned in to the thinking of the world. I was both human and angel. I walked in a garden without discomfort or despair. The sun dripped over everything, the flowers grew very high, a breeze blew gently, the water lapped softly. This was Eden in the early days of Creation. Adam and Eve were looking at me. I wasn't in the frame of the painting, but it was me they were looking at. I looked at the apple in her right hand and then I looked at her eyes.

It was a little after midnight when Sally was finally able to explain to me what had happened. We were both sitting on the bed. I was no longer hallucinating, but the sheets were almost unbearably white. Her naked body looked peach against the sheets. I was naked too. I felt very sad. It was the same feeling I always had when travelling home from family holidays: something was over; something had happened that would never happen again; people I had been happy with, I would never see again. I wanted to bury myself in the bed, cover myself in blankets and be seven years old again.

Chapter Eight

Friday.

I felt totally drained. Completely emptied out. It was as if I had poured myself in to a container and had somehow walked away from it.

This was meant to be a day off. But in the middle of a case like this, it was impossible to just take a day off. Always when you were least expecting it details would emerge, seeping into your thoughts until it become impossible to think of anything else.

But I had spent most of the day trying to stay away from the case. In the morning Andi had helped me sort out my mother's house. I was reluctant to sell, but we needed the cash. I now had the possibility of money, and it was only fair I contributed something to keeping the AndTom Detective Agency afloat. Andi wasn't pressing me, but we both knew it was the right thing to do. Nevertheless, selling the house would be like digging up a big chunk of the Renfield family tree. It foretold of a strange freedom. I suppose I'd always thought that one day I might return to live in the house.

We had lunch together outside Yates's Wine Lodge in Urmston. I wanted to be drunk. But I managed to resist. It was probably the after-effects of the acid. In the afternoon I ran a bath. I lay in the hot water, reading and thinking. I read the inside pages of an old copy of the local newspaper. Happy voices of children crept up from somewhere outside. I listened. I let the newspaper fall to the bathroom floor.

It opened on the front page, ***HORROR IN WILDERSPOOL WOODS***. It was a disturbing account of misery and death.

Police today launched a murder-style inquiry after a gruesome double death in Trafford. The investigation follows the discovery of a man's body in a blazing car in Wilderspool Woods. A woman, believed to be his common-law wife, was found with serious burns near a Ford Escort. The couple are thought to be postman Harry Bain and his girlfriend Susan Fern, who lived together with their two children in Kingsway Park, Davyhulme.

A neighbour said: 'They were a quiet couple but always seemed to be very happy. I just can't believe this has happened. It is so, so sad.'

The police first got involved when Susan's sister, Mrs. Crawford, reported that there had been a violent domestic dispute at the family home. When the police arrived, they discovered the living room heavily bloodstained. At 6.37pm the fire brigade was called to a car on fire in Wilderspool Woods, a mile from the family home. A woman had been seen staggering away from the blaze and after the fire was extinguished, a man's body was found in the boot of the car.

Paramedics gave emergency treatment to the woman, who was suffering from 80 per cent burns, but she died later in Withington Hospital. Officer Nigel French, of Urmston ambulance station, said: 'It was really horrific. The car was an inferno. No one could have survived the blaze. We did our very best. We administered treatment but the extent of her burns made it virtually impossible to save her.'

A team of detectives headed by Det. Supt. Tony Stockton, of Manchester CID, sealed off the area. Det. Supt. Stockton said attempts were being made to formally identify the body in the boot of the car from dental records. He added: 'This is a murder inquiry, and we are not seeking anyone else in connection with the deaths.' A neighbour, Michael Robinson, said he saw Susan Fern go out yesterday and return shortly afterwards with a wheelbarrow.

Neighbours said the couple had two children, a girl aged nine and a boy aged four, who are being comforted by relatives.

I finished the story, placed the newspaper back on the bathroom floor and closed my eyes for a moment. I emptied the bath, had a quick cold shower and then I got dressed. While I'd bathed, Andi had packed my mother's clothes.

When I joined her, Andi and I cleared drawers. It was mostly junk. My contribution came to a halt again when I discovered the book my mother had given me for my twenty-first birthday, *Your Mother's Manchester*. The book consists mostly of photographs of Manchester in the late 1950s.

I held the book and thought about my mother. I flicked through the pages until I found the photograph of Morton's Bookstall on Shudehill Market. We had talked about it many times, remembering the day she had first taken me there. I still had my 10p hardback copy of *The Poetical Works of John Keats*. Andi reassured me that it was safely packed away.

'To cease upon the midnight with no pain.'

Around five o'clock, in a hopeless attempt to escape the past, I did the twenty-minute walk to Barton Bridge to buy the Manchester Evening News. As I walked along on this bright April afternoon, the sun warming my back, I remembered a life once lived here at the mouth of the road: a boy with a head filled with impossible dreams and a handful of improbable friends.

Old Barton Road has been closed to through traffic for many years. Everywhere I looked was green or brown and overgrown. Vegetation was gradually engulfing and choking what had once been the main road between Urmston and Eccles. What used to seem permanent to a young boy in an old world, was either gone or going. The old school was now an establishment selling catering equipment. A 'For Sale' sign suggested that this change was itself soon to be overcome by further change. St Catherine's church had been demolished. The graveyard was barely visible, drowning beneath a sea of brown and green. As Professor Brian Fish might have said, the road had been culture imposed on nature; now, slowly, nature was regaining its hegemony. It made everything seem so temporary. It made me think, in a strange sort of way, of walking with my mother among the ruins of ancient Greece. The scale might be different, but the narrative was the same.

On returning to my mother's house, I glanced at my watch. I was surprised by how long I had been gone. What seemed like forty minutes was a little over an hour. How time passes when you're having fun.

I threw the unopened Manchester Evening News on the kitchen table.

'Would you like a coffee, Andi?'

'Yes. Then shall we eat?'

Without waiting for an answer, she picked up the Manchester Evening News and read the front page. She read the headline story carefully. She then turned to me, 'I think you should read this, Tom.'

She placed the newspaper on the table next to the two cups of coffee I had placed there. My eyes immediately fixed on the headline: ***ACADEMIC DIES IN GUNSHOT DEATH.***

I read the story straight through without stopping and without comment. What did it mean? The subheading, written in smaller print read: ***UNIVERSITY LECTURER FOUND DEAD. POLICE BELIEVE SUICIDE.***

When I had finished reading, I repeated the subheading three or four times in my head, 'University lecturer found dead.

Police believe suicide.'

The report told of how, late the previous evening, Dr William Warner, a senior lecturer in English at Manchester Metropolitan University, had been found dead in his Bolton home. The cause of death was a single blast from a shotgun. The police were not treating it as a suspicious death. No details of the circumstances of death were given.

The story quoted Professor Brian Fish. 'He was an outstanding literary scholar and a valued member of the academic community. He was writing a book that would have greatly influenced the teaching of literary studies for many years to come. He, and all the valuable work he would have undoubtedly produced, will be profoundly missed. He will be a great loss to the School of English.'

I felt numbed. I swallowed a mouthful of coffee and turned to Andi. Looking for relief, I asked, 'What do you think?'

A case can become like a smell, one gets used to it, no longer noticing it anymore. It takes someone new to detect it again. Andi is my olfactory aid. Not a title she likes or accepts. But when I can no longer see the significant details, she is able to make me refocus my critical gaze.

'He knew you were on to him. He killed himself to escape the law?'

'On to what?'

She knew it didn't make sense. She looked away, a little embarrassed.

Andi was not sure what to think. 'What do you think?'

'I don't know. I don't know. I'm just not sure. It doesn't make sense.'

I swallowed another mouthful of coffee. I had a headache coming on. I went into the kitchen to find some tablets.

'Would you like another coffee, Andi?'

'Okay,' she said, not too convincingly.

She followed me into the kitchen. We stood together by the table.

'There's always the possibility that Warner's death and Rebecca Morney's disappearance are not connected.'

Andi nodded. We looked at each other and smiled.

'It's not likely though, is it?'

But why was it not likely? We didn't know the answer.

Halfway through my second cup of coffee, my mood changed. 'Do you think I'm responsible?

'Responsible for what?'

'Maybe I'm not concentrating properly. I'm too preoccupied with my own problems. When I talked to him about Rebecca Morney, I probably opened the wound. He may have worried about what I might do with the information. He was obviously cut up about his relationship with Rebecca Morney. Remember, he is, I mean was, a very religious man.'

'But how does that make you responsible? Come on, Tom. It's not your fault. You didn't make him sleep with her. We don't even know if it's really connected with Rebecca Morney. And anyway, if you're going to think like that, blame Fish, he started the case.'

Blame Fish? I thought of Fish. Would he blame me? Had I misjudged his attitude to Warner? No. That was not possible. Fish spelled it out that he had no respect for Warner. He still might have liked him, though. He would not want him dead just because he wasn't a top academic like himself. And what about Rebecca Morney? Were the two events connected? This was the first case I'd worked on in which someone had died. I didn't like the feeling. Recovery and surveillance might be boring, but at least no one ever gets killed.

'What are you doing?' I asked, as Andi picked up the phone.

'I'm phoning for a pizza.' She started laughing. 'I'm phoning Carol at the Bolton Chronicle. She'll know more than we've just read in the Evening News. It might help.'

'It might help me stop feeling sorry for myself, you mean.'

'That as well,' she said. 'Look, someone has died. This is the first time anyone has died in any case we have worked. You are bound to feel a little responsible. I would feel the same. The feeling's only natural. But natural or not, and regardless of how you feel, you are not responsible. There is nothing you have done or said that would *cause* Warner to kill himself.'

Andi phoned Carol. Carol told Andi she would see what she could find out and phone back. Ten minutes later the phone rang. I took the call. Carol told me that the death had happened as reported in the Evening News.

'A neighbour discovered the body on his way to work. He'd been alerted by the noise.'

'The noise?'

'Yes. Warner's CD player was playing on repeat. The neighbour had woken to the music. Eaten breakfast to the music. Before leaving work, he knocked to complain. Getting no answer at the front of the house, he went around the back. It was then that he saw Warner lying dead on the kitchen floor. He was still holding the shotgun.

The neighbour phoned the police. The police came. They found nothing to make them suspicious. No sign of forced entry. Preliminary verdict: suicide.'

'Thanks, Carol.'

I was about to replace the phone when Carol added: 'There is one thing. Jim, who reported the case for us, says there was an old copper at the scene who thought that a couple of things were rather odd.'

'Yes?'

'There was no suicide note. Therefore, at the moment, no obvious motive.'

I made a mental note that the absence of a suicide note wasn't that uncommon. Then again, he was a literary scholar, a nineteenth-century literary scholar at that. He must have read hundreds of novels and short stories in which a suicide note was a significant feature? A suicide note would seem very likely with a man like Warner. Surely, he would want to leave some words. One would expect an explanation in his own words or, more cryptically, via a quotation.

Carol had already moved on. 'But more interesting than that, the angle of the wound doesn't seem quite right.'

'Not suicide?'

'Well, not yet. The official line remains that Warner killed himself, that it was in fact suicide. Jim says, it was just this one old copper who raised these doubts, unofficially. More of an aside, than an official statement or comment, you might say. But you know as well as I do how they work: asides have a way of working their way in to the mainstream of a case and becoming official.'

I nodded. I realised what I had done and said, 'Yes.'

'One other thing, Tom. Perhaps the real curiosity of the case.'

'Go on.'

'The music that alerted the neighbour. You know, the CD that was playing on repeat. It was Henryk Gorecki's Symphony No. 3. Do you know it?'

'Gorecki?'

'Yes. It was the best-selling classical record of last year.'

'What does it mean?'

'It makes me feel sad. But not that sad.'

'Carol, what's the significance of the music playing?'

'It was because it was this particular music that the neighbour was first alerted.'

'Why?' I asked, rather too incredulously.

'Because, clever clogs, Warner didn't have this CD.'

'Come on, Carol. How can the neighbour be so sure?'

'Well, he used to have the CD. But then he got rid of the CD, gave it to the neighbour who found the body. Apparently, the music carried too many bad associations.'

'Bad associations?'

'Yes. Bad associations. Associations of the worse kind, if you know what I mean.'

'Carol, what associations? Get to the point.'

'Okay. Gorecki was playing when Warner came home early one afternoon to find his wife rehearsing that scene from the remake of *The Postman Always Rings Twice*. Do you remember the scene? They do it on the kitchen table. Jack Nicholson and whatever she's called.'

'I think it was Jessica Lange.'

'Yes, I think you're right. Anyway, he walks in and wifey and neighbour are doing a perfect take.'

'Not the neighbour who found the body?'

'Great neighbours.'

'Not the same neighbour?'

'No, a different neighbour. Great neighbourhood, though. Anyway, the significant point is that he no longer had a copy of Gorecki's Symphony No. 3. As I said, he'd given his copy to the neighbour who found him dead.'

'I don't know what it means. But thanks, anyway. Before you go, give me the name and address of the neighbour who now owns the CD and found the body.'

She told me his address.

'See you soon. Bye.'

'And you. Oh, and give my love to Andi. See you both soon. Bye.'

'And thanks.'

'No problem. See you soon.'

I put down the phone and turned to Andi.

'About food,' Andi inquired, 'should I still phone a pizza place?'

'No. There's a pub just up the road. They do food. We can eat there.'

'What did Carol say?'

'She said Gorecki was playing on repeat when Warner's body was found. I'll tell you the rest in the car.'

The Swinging Bridge was a recent addition to the landscape of my childhood. I was having difficulty keeping my mind from wandering back to loss. Odd thoughts swelled in my head. Some memories are so solid, they are like places you feel that you might be able to return to one day. Even when my mother was visibly fragmenting, she still had a strange solidity I couldn't escape.

We had a quick meal. We then set off for Manchester. Andi had arranged to go for a drink with Lesley, the woman she likes to call her other partner. They have been living together for almost three years. Lesley's a wonderful person, but she doesn't like football. I once asked Andi how she could love someone who didn't like United. She gave the obvious answer: there is more to a relationship than liking the same things. I knew the answer very well. Most of my girlfriends had hated football.

I'd been invited to join them for a drink, but I figured I'd taken up too much of Andi's time lately. So, I declined. Anyway, I'd already made up my mind to talk to Warner's neighbour.

Chapter Nine

Driving to the centre of Manchester, Andi and I mulled over Carol's information. I tried some preliminary conclusions. 'Bill Warner committed suicide because he realised the gravity of what he'd done. He was a serious man, a religious man. He'd been celibate for almost two years before his brief encounter with Rebecca Morney. It was a commitment on his part. It must have felt like she mocked such commitments. He thought to kill her, but realised that it was he himself who was the guilty person. Always had been guilty. Rebecca Morney's safe now.

Oh my God, I suddenly thought, he had already killed her. She wasn't just missing, she was dead, murdered by Warner. That is why he had committed suicide. Andi agreed that this was a real possibility. It was what she had already suggested.

One thing that puzzled us both was why such a religious man as Warner would commit suicide. Surely, he would believe that it was better to suffer in silence and wait for the judgement of his God? Why put his soul at risk in this way? Had I misjudged his desperation?

I dropped Andi near Moseley Street Bus Station and continued across town and out to Bolton. It was just after eight o'clock when I arrived at Warner's house. I looked around. The sunlight and the flowers made it all look so peaceful. It should be damp with a light drizzle. The streetlamps should be struggling to penetrate the gloom. But instead of gloom there was just sunlight, flowers, and the sound of children playing and dogs barking. The scene was far too peaceful.

I parked across the road from the house. Looking at it I could see nothing to suggest the human tragedy that had been played out there less than ten hours earlier. I was not sure what I expected to see. I just felt that the house should stand out; look different from all the other houses. The enormity of what had taken place ought to be in some way articulated in the bricks and mortar. But what I was looking at was a very ordinary dwelling surrounded by a collection of other very ordinary dwellings that looked the same. The police tape was the only significant difference.

I reached into the glove compartment and pulled out a small leather wallet. I opened it and quickly flicked through the cards inside. I put them all back except one. I examined the phoney NUJ card. I turned it over in my hand. Being a private detective requires a certain talent for acting. Often the best way to get information is to pretend to be someone you are not. People like to talk to the press. Well, at least they like to talk to the press more than they like to talk to private detectives.

I knocked on the door of the neighbour who had found Warner's body. Next door, on the opposite side from Warner's, water from a garden sprinkler danced in the late evening sunlight. The smell of recently cut lawn filled my nostrils; a very attractive smell, making me think of happier times. A few doors down, there were a group of young men drinking beer and laughing about why they were trying to light a barbecue so late on an April evening. I wasn't hungry, but I could certainly drink a beer or two.

Mr Norman answered the door. He was in his early fifties. His build was athletic going to seed. Beneath his Bolton Wanderers football shirt, a beer belly was coming into full bloom. His breath told me it was a beer belly he was still working on. His expression was not particularly friendly.

I introduced myself as a reporter working for the Times Higher Educational Supplement. His expression became even less friendly. I told him I was trying to put together some background information for an article on why academics increasingly choose suicide. I had no idea if they did, increasingly or not, but it sounded like a good cover story.

'You didn't waste much time,' he said bluntly.

He invited me into a small front room; there was so much furniture in the room, it was difficult to manoeuvre. He directed me to a small sofa in the bay of the window. I struggled to make my way across the room, banging my knee painfully against the corner of a table. I don't know why, but I tried very hard to conceal the pain of my accident. If he noticed, he didn't say anything.

'Would you like a cup of tea, or something?'

I wanted to say, I'd have what he was drinking, but I said instead: 'Yes. A cup of tea would be wonderful.' It sounded more professional. But perhaps not very credible, given that I was pretending to be a journalist.

I talked in general terms about the pressures of academic life. I could see I was boring him. I kept suggesting that Warner must have been under a great deal of strain. Suicide was such a drastic solution to life's problems. He listened politely. But he seemed unconvinced. Eventually he interrupted me.

'It might not fit the angle of your story, young man, but I don't think academic life played any part in Bill Warner's death. It was his personal life that drove him to it.'

'What do you mean?,' I asked hopefully, trying not to sound too excited.

'His marriage was at the heart of it. Or rather it was his wife. She's a very beautiful woman. But she was never really a married woman, a real wife, if you know what I mean? Not what you would call a one-man woman, anyway.' He said the last sentence with a dark smile creeping across his large, shiny face.

I forced a smile and nodded. I swallowed a mouthful of tea. Norman drank deeply from a can of San Miguel. I then did what I always do in this kind of situation, I used flattery to gain information. They say flattery gets you nowhere, but I find that flattery usually works, it's philately that gets you nowhere. Andi had said this to me one night walking back from Old Trafford. I tried hard not to laugh as I remembered, knowing that laughing would make me seem weird, and worse, it would be counterproductive.

'If you don't mind me saying, you seem to be a man of great sensitivity, someone who can understand the suffering of others. Not many people even take the time to think about the feelings of others. You were obviously a very good neighbour.'

He accepted the compliments with a movement of his hands, a self-congratulatory smile, and a big gulp of beer. Whether he truly believed me, it had had the intended impact, he started to talk in more detail about Warner. I could almost hear the words beginning to accumulate in his head.

'What I'm about to say might sound awful. But it's common knowledge. I suppose that's part of the problem. Everyone knew what was going on. How she was carrying on. Some even joined in. Others would have liked to have joined in. Of course, Bill was the last to know. I wanted to say something. But it's so difficult. Sometimes it's harder to tell a friend, I suppose. I could never find the right words. Perhaps if I had, he might still be alive. I don't know.'

He paused for a moment, swallowing more beer, and thinking something over. It suddenly occurred to me that a genuine grief, perhaps even guilt, was driving his drinking. Perhaps he was a great deal more sensitive than I had given him credit for.

'They were always breaking up and getting back together. That was the awful and predictable pattern of their marriage. The last break up was the most serious. They must have been apart for about two years. Then they were back together again. Everyone was very surprised. What wasn't surprising was her behaviour. Back together or not, she continued where she'd left off.

'Look, I'm going to have another beer. Can I get you a beer instead of tea?'

'Yes, that would be great,' I said, trying not to sound too enthusiastic. 'Thanks,' I added.

His manner was no longer unfriendly. Yet still not what you would describe as welcoming. But he was proving to be a great source of information. I was beginning to feel a little guilty about my deception.

He left the room and returned with two bottles of beer. He passed one to me. Tsingtao. I was amazed. It was like what they say about buses: none and then two coming one after the other.

'Tsingtao beer?' I said, thinking I was suddenly surrounded by it.

'Yes. I first had it on a business trip to Shanghai. Now *there's* a place, one of the great cities of the world. Have you had it before?'

'Yes, but I had never had it until very recently. Great beer.'

'Yes,' he said and began to tell me about his time in Shanghai. Fascinating as this was, I needed to get him back to Warner.

'It sounds great. I've only heard great things about the place.'

Then I remembered. 'I think Warner spent some time in China. I think it said something about it in my briefing notes,' I added quickly, wondering if Warner had been there at the same time as Fish.

'Yes, he did,' he said rather dreamily. He was obviously finding it very hard to leave the Nanjing Lu and his first encounter with Tsingtao beer.

As if suddenly remembering why I was there, he changed the subject back to Warner and his unfaithful wife.

'That kind of betrayal can destroy a man. I had a friend in the army. We were stationed together in Malta. His wife committed suicide. He was heartbroken. We all rallied around while the army organised his transport home. We drank together. We got very drunk together. We did our best to console him. When he returned after the funeral, he was a different man. At first, we thought it was only natural. His wife was dead. We'd all be the same. Anyway, drunk one night, he told me how a couple of days after the funeral he had found his wife's diary. It explained in brutal terms the reason for her suicide. In terms so graphic, they were almost impossible for him to read and comprehend, and certainly never forget.

'She had killed herself because the man she loved would not leave his wife. The strange thing was that he said he now felt guilty for accepting our sympathy. He eventually drank himself out of the army.'

Then, as if responding to a question I had not asked, he said, 'I don't know what became of him after that. Perhaps he drank himself to death.'

He suddenly stopped talking, satisfied that he had made his point. What it was, I wasn't sure. But he had made it and that was all that mattered. I was beginning to wonder about his own marriage.

'Look,' he said, rather solemnly, 'I'm expecting my brother and his wife shortly. Is there anything more you need to know?'

I took a deep sip from my Chinese beer. 'Another reporter told me you said something about the music playing when Bill Warner's body was found.'

'I told him that Bill had given his copy of Gorecki's Symphony No. 3 to me after he'd come home early one afternoon to discover his wife and that bastard from number 8 at it in the kitchen. I've thought about it since I spoke to the reporter. I suppose Bill could have bought another copy. It may have been intended as a rather twisted suicide note, one last chance to punish his ex-wife. But somehow, I don't think so. I think it is a little suspicious.'

I thanked him and left.

Outside I deliberated about calling at number 8. What could I lose? I knocked on the door and waited. The door was opened by a tall man, with very short black hair. He had the look of an out-of-work actor. He smiled at me in a rather mocking way. He was obviously drunk.

'Hello. Sorry to disturb you, but I'm a reporter working for the Times Higher Educational Supplement. I was wondering if I could ask you some questions about the suicide of your neighbour Dr Bill Warner?'

'Did that nosey old woman Norman tell you to talk to me?' There was no sign of real irritation in his voice, only something resembling stage anger. 'It is that bastard Tony Grant who you should talk to. He's the man who is responsible. Blah, blah, blah. He should get a life of his own.'

'No, Mr Grant,' I said without a great deal of conviction. 'I'm trying to talk to as many neighbours as possible.'

'Are you sure Norman didn't send you,' he said, laughing.

'No, as I said, I'm a reporter with the Times Higher-'

Before I could say more, he said: 'Norman blames me for the end of Warner's marriage. He probably blames me for global warming. No doubt he thinks I am to blame for his suicide. Of course, I'm sorry that Warner is dead, but I am not to blame.'

'Why do you think he blames you?' I asked, rather disingenuously.

'I had an affair with Freda, Warner's ex-wife. Well, not an affair, I had sex with her a few times. I certainly wasn't the only one. Not even sure I was the only neighbour, including Norman. She was a very attractive woman. Not particularly good looking, but very sexual. Almost like an animal. I have never met a woman who was so sexually available, almost predatory. She was like a typical man, if you know what I mean?'

I nodded in encouragement. 'So why does Mr Norman blame you?'

'Why, because I was caught with her in Warner's kitchen. I'm not proud of myself. Obviously, I would rather it hadn't happened. Don't get me wrong, Mr Reporter, I'm not saying I wish I hadn't had sex with her. Sex with Freda was always fantastic. No, I just wish Warner hadn't found us together.'

'How did Warner react?' I asked, wondering if Grant might have had a more direct role in Warner's death.

'He just walked out and did not return to the house for

almost a week. Freda left him the day after he returned. I never spoke to her or him again. I saw him a few times, but he always ignored me, pretending I wasn't there. A real man would have confronted me.

'When I saw the young woman who visited him earlier on the day he killed himself, I thought he was coming around. You know what I mean? He chuckled softly. 'He was a lecturer, wasn't he? She was probably just a young student. But I did wonder why she was visiting him at home. I don't think that is normal, even for academic types.'

I nodded.

'She was certainly very attractive. Tall and slim, with thick brown hair tied back.'

My brain exploded into focus. Rebecca Morney?

'I think I may have interviewed her,' I said, trying to hide the lie. 'Tall, slim, almost skinny but with a distinct feminine form?'

'She was slim with big tits, if that's what you mean.'

I nodded again.

'I do remember that she had beautiful eyes and very thick dark eyebrows.'

'That's her,' I said. I was certain he was describing Rebecca Morney. So, she wasn't dead, Warner had not killed her. Why had she visited him? Had her visit pushed him over the edge?

'The guy with her wasn't so attractive.'

'She wasn't alone?' I asked, unnecessarily.

'She arrived with him in a green MG sports car. He was a tall, athletic guy, very posh. He waited in the car while she went in to see Warner. When she got back in the car, he got out and knocked on the door. Warner and the posh guy had a shouting match at the front door.'

'What were they arguing about?

'I couldn't hear properly. I just remember the guy's blond curly hair bobbing up and down as he shouted in a very posh voice at Warner. The young woman had to make him get back in the car. It didn't last very long. They got back in car and drove away. I thought I might have to intervene, if you know what I mean.'

I asked more questions, but got little additional information. Eventually Grant interrupted my line of questions with his own unease: 'I wish he had confronted me,' he said, his voice wobbling with regret amplified by alcohol.

'Who?'

'Warner, of course.'

I left Grant deep in darkening pools of remorse he was only just beginning to discover. I got back in my car and drove back to Hulme. I stopped once to buy two bottles of Australian dry white wine.

As I crossed the city centre, an ill-defined concern welled uneasily just below the surface of my consciousness. There was something I was missing, something not quite right, but I couldn't yet name it. I needed to sit down and review everything I now knew about the case. Make a list and study it carefully.

In bed I read T.S. Eliot. April is indeed the cruellest month. The thought welled up inside me and then I was asleep. I dreamed of a rose-garden and a woman with wet hair. Dead leaves were blowing across a vacant lot. She was standing alone, her arms outstretched, alone in a walled rose-garden. The background slowly dissolved. She was now standing in a vacant lot, her arms outstretched, her hands holding dead leaves. I articulated only one word: 'Why?' She tried to speak in response to my question, but her mouth gave up only bewilderment and fear. I awoke feeling bitterly cold and terribly alone.

Chapter Ten

Saturday morning.

I woke at 6.33. A neighbour's dog was barking aimlessly in a garden somewhere below. In the distance I could hear a car alarm. I washed and dressed. For breakfast, I ate toast made with brown bread and drank two cups of Kenyan medium roast coffee. I drank the second cup of coffee on the small balcony outside the kitchen. I leaned on the wrought iron railing and listened, half-expecting to hear the build-up of the morning traffic below on Cambridge Street and the Mancunian Way. The traffic was mostly hidden from view by three large and leafy sycamore trees. On a weekday, in less than two hours, the traffic would reach its rush-hour crescendo.

The sunshine played through the green leaves, making some glow almost yellow. The leaves sparkled and fluttered in the gentle breeze. It was like being in the moment as Renoir prepared to put paint on canvas. But I couldn't help but think of autumn.

My plan was to arrive in Whitby at around lunchtime, see the sights and then retire with a few bottles of beer to my hotel room at some time shortly before 3.00 and listen to Radio 5's coverage of United's game against Ipswich Town.

Sally had suggested that Rebecca's mother might be able to help. I had been very tempted to invite Sally to accompany me to Whitby. But I wasn't sure what she would say. In the end I decided it would only complicate things. Don't mix business with pleasure, as they say. My problem, among many others, was that

I wasn't sure if it was business or pleasure. Only time would tell.

I'd arranged to see Mrs Morney at 10.00 on Sunday morning. It was a Bank Holiday weekend, but she said she'd see me anyway. I'd stay in Whitby overnight and then continue to Staithes the following morning. Andi had advised me that a little tourism would do me good. It would take my mind off other things.

'Have a few drinks, take a walk on the beach, talk to the sea, that kind of thing. It will be good for you.'

Andi had been advised to do something similar when her brother had been kicked to death by racists in the street battles between left and right in late-seventies Manchester. Joe had not been right nor left, just black. His skin colour signed the death warrant of a pointless and brutal death. When the police called Andi to identify his body, he had been beaten so badly she hardly recognised him. He was so disfigured; she had hoped against hope that it wasn't Joe. But it was Joe. No one was ever charged with his murder.

I left the apartment at 7.10, arriving at my mother's house at 7.35. I collected what I came for and left. The traffic on the M63 was very light, even for a Saturday morning.

I thought about Warner as I passed the sign for the Bolton turn-off. I thought about him again when I saw the sign for Hartshead Moor and its associations with Chartism. To tell the truth, I hardly stopped thinking about him. At least it prevented me from dwelling morbidly on other problems. Every cloud, as they say.

Crossing Saddleworth Moor, the rain thickened. The moor looked bleaker than usual in the rainy mist. This was a place of dark and disturbing secrets. The moor and its terrible murders had become embedded in so many unconnected family histories. I can still remember my mother and neighbours, many years later, discussing the events as if they touched them directly. The absolute horror of the murder of children put the Rebecca Morney case into very cold perspective.

I stopped the car at Ferrybridge Services at 8.55. I drank

two cups of coffee. Between cups, I scrutinised a large close-up photograph of lettuce leaves, hanging opposite my table. I was thinking about Warner's death again. But I was trying hard not to. I'd read somewhere that the colour green is soothing on the eyes. What about the mind? I asked, almost audibly.

I sat in the car park with a 1991 edition of the AA Road Atlas of Great Britain on my lap, deliberating which way to go. I finally decided on the A170. It promised the most interesting scenery. I left the car park at 9.50.

I turned off the A1 on to the A168. I quickly became preoccupied with the names of the villages. Strange sounding names, Dishfort, Asenby, Baldersby St James, Sessay, Toncliffe. They all sounded like names from a nineteenth-century novel. Yes, the kind of novel Warner would read and teach. He was back in my head again.

I missed the turning for the A170. Warner again. Rather than turn back, something I have an almost pathological dislike of doing, I continued along the A19, turning off on to the A172, and then the A173. At Great Ayton, I was unsuccessfully tempted by a large sign advertising the Captain Cook Monument. I joined the A171 at Guisborough, where I stopped for petrol. I arrived in Whitby just before noon.

My hotel overlooked the cold, grey North Sea. I unpacked my small black suitcase, put the toiletries in the bathroom, my clothes in the drawers and wardrobe and threw Engels' *The Condition of the English Working Class* in England on the bed. I remembered being drunk in the Lass O'Gowrie with Andi. When she arrived, I was reading it. She said I was trying too hard to be a student again. I showed her the book.

'I am reading about Manchester and Salford in the nineteenth century. I promised Auntie Hetty I would do a little background research for her. She is doing the Renfield family tree.'

'Yes, I know. How's it going?'

'We came from the Yorkshire Dales. We arrived in Manchester, via Leeds, in the 1830s. Auntie Hetty will not be happy when I tell her what Engels has to say. She was so pleased that we had lived in the Yorkshire Dales and thinks that coming to Manchester must have been even better.'

'Having been to Yorkshire, I think she is right.'

'Read what he says, and you will realise how awful their lives must have been.'

'My ancestors were slaves. In fact, the exploitation of my ancestors financed the exploitation of your ancestors.'

We spent most of the evening getting drunk and worrying about our ancestors. We were trying to remember what Walter Benjamin had said.

From the second window of my hotel room, I could see the River Eske and next to it Whitby's main street. The street was busy with tourists. They walked up and down, looked in windows, and went in and out of shops and cafes. There was a great deal of happy laughter. I decided to join them.

I had lunch in a pub near the harbour. About halfway through the meal, my eyes wandered to another table. A man and woman were sitting in silence. He stared at his food, concentrating fully on the movement of his knife and fork from plate to mouth. She had stopped eating and stared at her reflection in the window. From outside they would look like a scene from an Edward Hopper painting. Was this the end of something or the beginning of something? As I turned away, I knew again why I had wanted to become a detective. It was a stupid thought, but better than most of the thoughts I had had recently.

No longer hungry and slightly drunk, I spent a couple of hours looking around the town. I played the good tourist. I did a little sightseeing, a little window shopping, and then I bought an ice cream and walked on the beach. It was like being in Wales again. Every year as a child, my mother and I had gone to Wales. We always stayed in a caravan, and we always spent most of our time on the beach. The only real exception was visiting castles. I had a little guidebook to castles in Wales, which I carried with me everywhere. Each year I would tick those I had visited. My mother loved photography. 'Go there, Tommy! Smile, Tommy! That will make a wonderful picture, Tommy.' The blow of being back at home was always softened by the arrival of the photographs: Tommy by the castle gate; Tommy at the drawbridge; Tommy running headlong into the waterless moat; Tommy in the sea; Tommy eating ice cream on the beach.

I went into a small cafe near the river. I ordered a pot of tea for one and two toasted teacakes. A radio was playing pop music I didn't recognise. It made me feel old. As I ate my second toasted teacake, Judy Garland began to sing a live version of *Somewhere Over the Rainbow*. It was very beautiful and reminded me of something in my childhood. I knew it was more than just watching the *Wizard of Oz* at Christmas with my mother, but what that the something more was, I could not tell. An old man in his late seventies began to sing along. He seemed completely oblivious to the cafe's staff or to its other customers. He sang quietly with determination until the song finished. He then paid his bill and left quickly, tears in his eyes, as if in a hurry to be somewhere else. I watched him through the window walk at great pace across the street and then across the bridge. I lost him amongst the many people bobbing in and out of shops.

At 2.50 I left the little cafe and returned to my hotel and listened to the radio coverage of United's game against Ipswich Town. It was a hard-fought match. A goal down after 19 minutes, United equalised through Cantona in the 36th minute. Giggs hit the winner two minutes after half-time. United's lead was now five points over Blackburn with two games remaining. The league title was almost won. The only worry was the injury to Schmeichal. He looked certain to miss the Cup Final. I mumbled the disappointment to myself.

I looked down from the small window. People were moving in the street below, some towards the beach, some towards the bridge. A mixture of colours and shapes forming and reforming. Here was art. As Andi was fond of saying, especially when drunk, *the aesthetic is just a way of seeing.*

I went out and bought fish and chips. I sat on the harbour wall, and I watched the sun burn a golden line into the cold grey North Sea. I tried hard to think about United, but my mother would not leave me alone. Eventually, Warner came back and then Rebecca Morney. Dark eyes: pools of sadness against a background of frozen traffic. Why was Fish paying me to find her?

I started to walk back to the hotel as the sun started to set behind Sandsend Ness. Then I changed my mind. In the April evening stillness, I walked back to the beach. I walked for a long time along the quiet shoreline. Occasionally I kicked out without purpose at a pebble or a shell, lifting sand into the deepening gloom.

I tried hard to think about football, about United, about the game against Ipswich, about Gigg's winning goal, about the Premier League title, about anything and everything. But all I could think about was a woman I had loved until she died - loved her to death. And yet I had not loved her enough. I knew that now. It is so easy to know things when knowing them no longer makes any difference.

Eventually I found a pub. I walked in and felt the warmth and the music surround me. A local band was playing. I bought a pint and found a seat near the window. It was now raining outside. I listened to the music while watching the rain forming patterns on the River Eske.

When the band stopped to take a break, I took out my notebook and began to review the Rebecca Morney case. Fish wanted to find Rebecca Morney. Warner had had an affair with her. Trelawny behaved a little strangely when we met at the university. Warner was now dead. Probably suicide. Rebecca Morney and a friend had argued with Warner the day he died. Guy fancied Rebecca Morney, but she didn't fancy him.

Guy spiked my drink with acid, and I don't know why. Sally? Sally helped me. Would she offer further help? Mrs Morney? Would she know where to find her daughter? Would she help? Reviewing the case, I realised my notes consisted mostly of questions. There was one key question that I was no nearer answering than I had been at the beginning of the case: where is Rebecca Morney and why is she missing? I closed my notebook and returned it to my inside pocket.

As I was buying my third pint, the band began again. The pub was quite full now. There is something about live music, even if it is not very good. This band, however, were good. Too old to be thinking of making it big, they were nevertheless good musicians who knew how to entertain. As I watched and listened, I wondered if they had got close to success when they were younger. Dreams of stardom had long gone, now replaced by a certain pride in playing well regardless of when or where the performance. There is a certain kind of purity in playing because you like playing. I loved what I heard and stayed in the pub until closing time.

It was very dark on the beach. The wind was cold and unwelcoming. I buttoned up my brown suede jacket and walked towards the sea. The band had done a great version of 'Who'll Stop the Rain.' Without thinking about it, I started to sing some of the words as I walked on the beach. I cut between verses, back and forwards, finding it very difficult to hold the tune.

I suddenly felt so very lonely. The waves curled and fell. It was like watching an invading army. I stood alone, the only witness to the invasion. I knew I wasn't going to warn anyone. Rain began to fall even more heavily. I was soon very wet.

I stood in the centre of the old bridge, my hands gripping the cold railings, and I watched as the river flowed beneath me down to the sea. The river trembled as the darkness closed in on it. I looked down at the navigable channel and I wondered if it was as deep as the water I was standing in. I looked down at the dark surface of the river. Shadows dipped deep into the cold, dark water. For a moment I imagined what might happen if I followed them. The river was flowing darkly like her hair. I wanted her close to me. I wanted to feel her hair in my face. I wanted her to take my photograph. I just wanted her to be alive. I was crying. My tears were falling into the river. My tears were flowing down to the sea. They were lost in the flow of the water. 'Fuck off, God,' I shouted in desperation.

Walking back to the hotel, I started to laugh. Once back in my room, I dried myself and I listened to the falling rain beat out an inviting rhythm against my window. Outside the rain drifted seaward and windows glowed yellow in to white, presenting only weak resistance to the surrounding darkness.

I opened the window wide and breathed in the cool damp air. Below, a small fishing boat, with glowing red and blue lights, moved slowly down the river towards the open sea. I could hear voices, one old and one young, but I couldn't make out what they were saying. I closed the window and got ready for bed. I lay in the dark thinking about what I would say to Mrs Morney.

It was a long time before I fell asleep. I was not expecting good dreams. I wasn't disappointed.

Chapter Eleven

Sunday morning.

I woke up at exactly 5.17. I hadn't slept well. Even on holiday, it usually takes me a few days to settle into a new bed. I made coffee and watched the sun rise over the North Sea. Should I go for a walk along the beach; allow the sea breeze to blow away all my troubles? The prospect reminded me of how tired I was. I got back in bed and dozed for another two hours.

I looked in the bathroom mirror. Any resemblance to my young self was fading fast. I seemed to have aged about ten years in the last few months. The bags under my eyes would no longer pass as hand luggage. I splashed cold water on my face. I watched the water slip through my fingers, an action that seemed to repeat. It felt cold and that was that. I shaved, showered, and dressed quickly.

I had breakfast around 8 o'clock. Instead of my usual toast or cereal, I had bacon, sausage, egg, mushrooms, and tomatoes. It tasted good. I drank two cups of coffee. The coffee was not so good. I drank a glass of grapefruit juice to get rid of the taste of the coffee. A little hung-over, but I was ready for the world.

It was a dry, bright day. I left the hotel at around 8.45. Not as warm as it had been of late. The temperature was not helped by the wind coming in off the North Sea. I bought the Sunday Times at a shop near the harbour. The headline cheered me: ***BIG WIN IN SIGHT FOR THE ANC***. I knew Andi would be preparing for a party and I wanted to be there.

I walked across the bridge into the old town. I had time to spare, so I found a cafe. I ordered coffee. It was much better than the coffee in the hotel. The paper's main front-page story predicted the ANC would gain 54.7% of the vote. I read the report and then turned to the sport's pages. Smiling, I read the report of United's 2-1 victory against Ipswich Town. This gave United a five-point lead over Blackburn Rovers. The championship must surely be ours again. We'd waited so long and now champions in successive seasons, it was like a dream. Sometimes it was hard to believe. Andi and I repeated this thought to each other so often it was beginning to sound like a Buddhist mantra.

I left Whitby at 9.30 and arrived in the long stay car park above the village of Staithes at just before 10.00. The map had said the road between Staithes and Whitby was an A road, but for most of the early part of the journey it drove like a B road. For a time, I thought I was on the wrong road.

Four to twenty-four hours for £3, so I put three one-pound coins in the slot and pressed the button for the ticket.

Walking back to the car, I noticed the potash mine across the valley. Chimneys puffing, it looked incongruous, a grey moment in a bright passage of green. I could see people working. Voices echoed across the valley. I could make out only odd words. But the laughter was unmistakable. There was also the sound of heavy machinery, but even that could not block the sound of laughter.

I took out my notebook to review what I knew so far. It wasn't very much. As I walked down the hill I began to rehearse the questions I would ask Mrs Morney. It was even possible that Rebecca Morney might be here. Probably not, I conceded a little reluctantly.

Soft white lumps of cloud drifted slowly across the sky. At school I had completed a project on clouds, but as I stared upwards, nimbus or cumulus, I couldn't be sure. But what I did know was that if I stared long enough I would see recognisable shapes.

The air was soft and warm. It seemed to hold me as I made my way down the hill. I remembered Desert Island Discs. It was the only radio programme I tried not to miss. My regret at missing it was softened by my remembering that that day's islander was an explorer. Someone had once told me that explorers are like detectives. I strongly disagreed. We do things for other people; explorers are just rich people who do it all for themselves. In the soft warm air, I was prepared to concede that I had been a little too dogmatic in my argument.

I found the house easily.

The Morney's property (this seemed the most appropriate term) was a stone house called Rockshore Cottage, overlooking where the river meets the harbour. It wasn't large, but it did stand out, imposing itself on the local scenery. Solid and commanding, it seemed to emanate from out of the physical landscape itself.

I looked at the sea and then at the river. The tide was out. Fishing boats were lying stranded in the shallow water. Men, mostly old and sea-worn, smoked and talked and waited. The sun shone down on the river. It sparkled like so many silver coins. One of the men started laughing.

I knocked. I was about to knock again when Mrs Morney opened the heavy wooden door. It creaked and moaned, framing the unsteady figure of Mrs Morney. Standing with her hand on the doorknob, she opened her mouth without speaking. I introduced myself. She seemed a little surprised. I reminded her of our telephone conversation. She smiled and opened the door wide to allow me to enter.

She must have been in her late forties. But she looked very young. She had obviously been a very beautiful young woman. Although she was no longer beautiful, she was still very attractive. Her thin, pale green dress gripped her slim but shapely body. Her eyes were dark and penetrating like her daughter's. She also had the same thick black hair. In fact, the more I looked at her the more it seemed I was looking at an older version of the woman I had seen in the photograph Fish had brought to my office on the first day of the case. I know that daughters look like their mothers, but the similarity was striking.

Once we were inside, she was more welcoming. 'Would you like a drink?' she asked.

'Coffee, please,' I replied.

'Coffee? Would you like something stronger?' she said, almost teasing.

She waved a half-empty glass in my general direction. I ignored it. I wanted to draw her attention to the time of day, but I resisted the temptation to do so.

'No. Coffee's fine,' I said. 'Thanks.'

I noticed again that her body swayed a little unsteadily. She was obviously a little drunk. I couldn't help looking at my watch again. Stop it, I said to myself. It might make it easier. Drunk or not, her movements were now like dance steps. The choreography might have been induced by alcohol, but it was graceful, coquettish, and compelling. I watched the performance as she made me a cup of coffee.

Just as quickly as she had fixed my fascination, her mood suddenly changed. She became slow and gloomy. And then, as if from somewhere dark and deep inside, her voice began to shape disturbing and deliberate words. At first they conjured up situations that didn't seem to make much sense.

Gradually the words formed into a recognisable narrative. 'It was a brief, unthinking affair. That's what he said. I believed him. There seemed no point in not believing him. After all.'

Her voice just trailed off. She moved to the window. She pulled a curtain to one side. Was she watching the fishermen? It suddenly seemed important to know. I tried unsuccessfully to follow the direction of her gaze.

As if to answer my pointless curiosity, she said: 'The tide is coming in now. The men will soon be free to fish the sea. But it was an affair and not quick, casual sex. I suppose it was *that* that really hurt, it was *that* that really hurt me.'

I could see that she found it painful to recall. But I still had no idea what she was talking about. She continued, 'He ended it. I don't know why. He never said. I never asked. He ended it. But she wanted it to continue. She tried to keep the connection going. You know; notes, letters, phone calls, confrontations in the street. I would have probably done the same,' she said with a certain forced generosity, like an actor stepping out of character to offer clarification.

'Anyway, it gradually stopped. The connection gradually became severed. Then after six months or so, she wrote that she had to speak to him. He ignored the letter's plea. Then she phoned him. It was very important that she speak to him. Couldn't speak over the phone, it had to be face to face. At first, he refused. But she insisted. She assured him that she didn't want to start the affair again. But she had to speak to him. So, he arranged to meet her. She suggested a pub on the moors, The Legendary Saltergate Inn. What she had to tell him was important. She kept stressing that it was very, very important indeed.'

I asked if I might open a window. I had suddenly noticed how oppressively claustrophobic the room had become. She moved to the window, overlooking where the river meets the harbour, and opened it wide. The curtains fluttered in the light spring breeze. I took a deep breath. So did Mrs Morney. The sound of her breathing echoed with the sound of the gulls outside the window. She didn't speak, but she seemed to tremble as if swayed by the breeze.

'They sat down with drinks. She took a mouthful of Chardonnay and came straight to the point. She was already tearful when the first words came out. She was hysterical when she had finished what she had come to say to him.'

I caught her glance and tried to smile.

'This is how I was told the story, anyway.'

The curtains flew up against the top of the window frame. There was a sudden burst of laughter from below, followed by the mournful sound of gulls.

'It was not a ploy to re-establish their relationship. It was something he needed to know. She had been ill, fever, tiredness, headache, that sort of thing. She thought it was flu. She went to see her doctor. Through instinct or caution, or perhaps because of a recent bombardment of material, he advised a test. She was counselled and eventually took the test. She was told she was HIV Positive. It took a few days before she realised that *my* husband needed to know.'

Mrs Morney poured herself another drink. This time she didn't offer me one. She sipped and sipped and continued her narrative. 'He told me that same evening, first the betrayal, then the death sentence. I don't know what stopped me from killing him as he staggered around the room, taking large mouthfuls of vodka and saying how sorry he was.'

She stopped speaking and finished her drink. She poured herself another. Soon she would be incoherent, I thought.

'Why hadn't he taken precautions? There'd been enough warnings in the press and on the TV. He said he had, except one time. She wanted to feel him inside her, you know, without.'

She was shouting now. 'I didn't want to hear the intimate details. How could he tell me that?'

As Mrs Morney told more and more of her story the struggle against tears became more and more hopeless. I waited, unsure of what more to do. I began to wonder how long she had been drinking.

'We actually made love that night. Can you believe that?'

I tried but I couldn't.

'It's another illusion. We didn't make love, we did what we always did, I opened my legs, and he masturbated inside me. I wanted to ask if it was like that with her. I wanted to ask but I couldn't. I had never met her, but we were now on death row together.'

Mrs Morney started crying. I rose from my chair and approached her. She needed help. But what could I do? I asked about her doctor. She pointed to a cork notice board in the kitchen. I phoned and explained. The doctor was on his rounds. A secretary promised to page him. I got the sense this would not be his first visit. I returned from the kitchen with a pot of tea. When Mrs Morney saw what I was carrying she laughed, a bitter, hollow laugh.

'I want a drink. If you want to help, pour me another drink.'

I hesitated. What the hell, I thought. Given what had happened, who was I to play the puritan. I poured two large vodkas.

'I've not taken the test yet. I don't know if I ever will. What is the point?'

For a split second, I wondered what I'd do. I had no idea. Instead, I gulped at my vodka. It was very cold. I remembered Poznan. But it had no relevance here, so I pushed it away.

Almost speaking into her glass, she began again. 'The worst was telling Rebecca. She wouldn't believe it at first. When she did, she took it very badly. It overwhelmed her like a strange madness. She went very quiet for a long time. Wouldn't speak at all. Then she exploded in rage. She hated Michael, then she blamed me. It was devastating, worse, in a weird way, than the consequences of Michael's betrayal. We had always been a very close family, you see; very close, very loving, a single unit. Always of one.'

Mrs Morney seemed to be using words to bring it all back again. If she could get the correct words and the syntax right, she might get the past right. The thought appealed to me.

'This destroyed all that. There was no oneness anymore. The more we tried, the more our efforts seemed hollow and pointless, even a little cruel. The family had been sentenced to death on the floor of his office, in the back of his car, in a cheap motel on the edge of some Midlands town. On the-'

She was crying again, loud sobs, accompanied by the free flow of tears running down her cheeks.

'What am I saying? It's all fantasy. The long goodbye would be an apt description of our relationship, one long goodbye from beginning to end. We were students together. We met on a theatre visit to London. Before we got together, I remember how, on one night, we were in the hotel bar after a performance. He was very friendly with a woman behind the bar. Casual became serious all too quickly. It was a performance, probably better than the one we'd paid to see. I knew then that he had the capacity to hurt people - to hurt me, I mean. Love can be a terrible thing. It drives you on regardless of the dangers clearly indicated all along the way. All that bullshit about fools rushing in is fucking true.'

Mrs Morney walked to the window. Another gull broke into a moan. As if continuing a habit of a lifetime, she seemed to wait for the gull to be silent, then she spoke again. 'I soon got sick of all his guilt. He wore it like a fucking badge. It was as if he thought his guilt made everything okay. I am a victim and being a victim means never having to really say I'm fucking sorry - and mean it. It was all written on his fucking badge in capital letters.'

She crossed and re-crossed the room.

'At least you are safe, Rebecca.' He said the words not to comfort her, but to parade his guilt. Rebecca responded with outrage. She was hysterical. She accused him of imposing an exclusion zone. She said he was saying there was a circle of pain from which she was excluded. He tried to explain. I tried to explain. She only screamed about being rejected. If we wanted to shut her out, well, so fucking what, she was glad to be excluded. She kept saying this is not my fucking family anymore. It was the first time I had ever heard her swear. She hurled a coffee cup, smashing it against the wall, and stormed out. I have not seen her since that day.'

'Do you think her father would know where she is?'

'I doubt it. Don't be fucking stupid. Did you not hear what I just said? I thought you were a fucking detective?'

I said I was sorry for being so naive, so insensitive.

In a moment of calm, she said: 'He's working in Newcastle

at the moment.'

She made a gesture of inverted commas when she said the word working.

'Do you have his address?'

'He has a house in Whitburn. He'll be staying there.'

She reached for her bag.

'You know you cannot repress unhappiness; it continually returns as other people's unhappiness. The unhappiness that is visited on us, we visit on others. Perhaps we don't know we're doing it, but we do it all the same. We made our pain her pain. We made her feel our pain. Then we told her she did not feel a thing. That's a terrible thing to do to your own daughter. That was the worst thing we did.'

She was already blaming herself for Rebecca's pain. All those middle-class expectations had come down to this. Middle-class dreams slipping away into nothingness. Walking her to school for the first time. Helping her with her homework. Cheering her on at every sports day. Negotiating with teachers about the real meaning of her academic performance. Which university? What career? A golden fortress made of middle-class dreams now lay in ruins. I could see that it was very hard to take.

She removed a pen and a small notebook from her bag. She wrote down the address of Michael Morney's house in Whitburn. She handed it to me, and I put it in my inside pocket. I had no idea if I would ever go to Whitburn. Mrs Morney was obviously right, Rebecca Morney would not be there.

She placed the bag on a table near the window. It looked like a souvenir from North Africa. A token of better times. She turned it over. Her hand searched again in its deep interior. The bag was woven from brightly striped fabric. Her hand emerged with a soft black leather wallet. As she withdrew it, a random assortment of other items toppled out on to the sofa and on to the floor.

As I started to pick them up, she shouted, 'Leave them. They are not important.' Then, no longer shouting, she said, 'I'll pay whatever it costs to find Rebecca. Tell me the rate. I'll pay it. I'll pay more. I just want to find her.'

'I'm already being paid to find Rebecca. As I said on the phone, the university hired me to find your daughter.'

'I don't give a fucking shit about that,' she said savagely. 'Rebecca's my daughter. If she's lost, I'm the person who pays to find her.'

Mrs Morney carefully wrote out a blank cheque and placed it in my hand. The gesture was, for me, purely symbolic. I took it, folded it in half and placed it carefully in the pocket of my thick, white cotton shirt. I would send it back at a later date. If she still insisted on payment, I would send the money to the Terence Higgins Trust or some other such charity.

'The last time I saw her it was raining. I caught the door as she tried to slam it. She looked lost and alone. I tried to stop her, to comfort her, but she said it was too late for that. I watched her walk away until she disappeared into the rainy darkness. She had briefly looked back over her shoulder. I could see that there were big teardrops in her dark, sad eyes. I felt so useless, so guilty and so hopeless. Do you know what it's like to be without hope?'

I didn't answer.

Remembering had produced its expected result: she was crying again. 'You must let me know the minute you find her. You understand?'

Her voice was resonating with the kind of desperation alcohol only amplifies. In my head I heard Fish make the same demand, 'You must let me know the minute you find her. The minute. I mean it. Do you understand?'

I nodded.

She stood up unsteadily and turned on the TV. A man handed something to a woman. She turned away and then turned back and smiled. I couldn't quite make out the conversation that followed. Seemingly satisfied, she turned off the TV and returned to her chair.

She poured herself another drink. Where was the doctor? I considered phoning again.

'Do you know the legend of the two mermaids? It's a local legend,' she added, as if this would jog my memory.

I told her that I had never heard the story.

'A very long time ago, two mermaids came ashore at Staithes and were made prisoners by two local men. When the mermaids escaped back to the sea, they put a curse on the village. According to the curse, the day will come when the sea reaches Jackdaw's Well.'

She remained silent for a long time. Then she got herself another drink. Again, she didn't offer me one. She seemed oblivious to my presence. I sat there quietly as she talked to herself. I couldn't complain, I'd talked to myself a lot lately.

At last, the doctor arrived. I briefly explained the situation and left patient and doctor alone together. I walked back up the hill out of Staithes. Being a private detective has a way of making you incline towards pessimism. You must work hard at optimism. Mrs Morney would have to work very hard indeed. I wondered if she would now take the blood test.

I walked up the hill back to the car park. I glanced back at the sea. A dark mist was engulfing the village. The sea mist followed me up the hill. I got in my car and turned on the lights to begin the three-hour drive back to Manchester.

Obviously I hadn't really looked, but there'd been little sign of the Staithes Group, a community of painters regarded by their contemporaries in the late nineteenth century as radical modernists. There was little to report back to Andi, at least not on that front. I remembered bits from Andi's briefing. Frederick William Jackson, a leading member of the group, had studied at the Manchester School of Art.

I didn't start the car. I was having difficulty keeping my focus fixed firmly on driving. The air was damp and the sea mist was still moving up the hill. The day was getting dark far too early.

Besides the noise of very occasional traffic, there was only the sound of seagulls. I thought of how only rhymed with lonely.

I got out of the car and walked to the edge of the car park. I sat on a rock and looked back in the direction of Staithes. The fading lights were swimming in my eyes. I remembered the print Andi had shown me. An example of the work of the Staithes Group, it was a painting by Robert Jopling called 'A Lover and His Lass.' A young woman and a man, sitting together on the grassy cliff above the village; in the estuary below, a fishing boat heads out to sea. There are other couples and other boats, but the focus is this couple and this boat. For a moment the image seemed to clarify everything. Here was a material reality on which I could fix my critical gaze.

I was being engulfed by a sad and sullen sea mist. I could smell the dampness on the earth and grass. I could feel the wet air on my face. It was like being kissed by a lover I no longer loved, had probably never loved.

For a few moments I sat quietly. I longed for silence, a nothingness without demands. I studied the falling mist surrounding me. I heard a dog barking. Far away I heard some men shouting. But mostly I heard seagulls. Then I thought I could hear a woman's voice. Was it Mrs Morney calling for my help?

I watched the mist move across the sky. I watched as white became light grey, and then dark grey, and dry became wet. Without thinking, I searched for the morning in the coming darkness. As with any problem, the first thing to be established are the questions. I was a little confused.

Looking away from the village, I noticed something by the edge of a group of trees. It was a rabbit. I walked over and I reached down to make sure it was dead. Without thinking about what I was doing, I picked it up. The body was still warm. I walked back with it to the rock, found some soft ground and dug a small grave. Mostly with my bare hands, I buried the rabbit. Imperceptibly but inexorably, the tears began to form.

I cried wet and loud at the burial of an unknown rabbit. Well, not quite unknown; it was the rabbit who said his prayers to a rainbow in Rimbaud's poem. Without a rainbow to pray to, I was talking to the trees, to the flowers, to the bruised sky, to the hidden sun, moon, and stars. I was talking to anything but myself. I wanted to be far away, in a place where I didn't have to talk to anything or anyone.

I waited in the wet darkness. I was kneeling, praying like a rabbit for a rabbit, addressing a rainbow that I knew would never come. I held a handkerchief against my face. I could not remember removing it from my pocket.

I thought I heard the croak of a frog. I resisted the temptation to find it, to place a hopeful kiss.

It was almost completely dark when I got back in the car, unnaturally dark. The lights of Staithes blinked back at me in the distance. I thought about phoning Andi. But I knew what would happen. I would tell her about Mrs Morney and about the rabbit, and she would tell me it was really something else. There would be sympathy and understanding, lots of it, but knowing it was displacement wouldn't really help.

In the rear-view mirror, the town dropped behind the horizon. It had disappeared without trace, lost in sea mist, as if it and its occupants had never existed. I remembered the legend of the mermaids and tried to smile. Here was a fantasy that might even bring comfort to Mrs Morney.

A Drowning Man

Chapter Twelve

Without giving it any real thought, I turned the car around and headed back towards Whitby. I had decided that another night away from Manchester was probably the best plan. I justified it to myself by planning to visit Whitburn in the morning. I wasn't sure what I would gain from seeing Mr Morney, but I was so near I might as well take the chance. I had so little to lose.

As I approached the roundabout just outside Whitby, I saw a sign for Robin Hood's Bay. I decided I would find a hotel there.

The day was bright again. The sea mist had disappeared as quickly as it had arrived. I felt a sudden upsurge of optimism.

Up Prospect Hill, I passed what seemed like rather forlorn looking Victorian guesthouses. Down the hill and over the bridge spanning the River Eske, on the left was Whitby and on the right the Eske Valley emerging from the North Yorkshire Moors. I followed the A171 for Scarborough for a couple of miles and then turned left on to a B road dropping slowly to Robin Hood's Bay. I passed the Seaview Caravan Park and the lambs in the fields, and the fields of bright yellow rape seed. Here everything seemed more cheerful in the gentle breeze and the late afternoon sunshine. Feelings of springtime grew upon me the closer I got to Robin Hood's Bay. It was almost like being on holiday.

Rather than attempt to drive into the old fishing village, I parked my car in the first car park sign posted. It was the Station Car Park, but the railway station had long gone. It was now, rather quaintly, the Village Hall. I paid £2 for a four-hour stay and began my search for a hotel.

I looked down at the village. A fistful of mostly red-topped houses pressed between moor and sea. The Grosvenor was the first hotel. I kept walking down the steep slope toward the centre of the old fishing village. The White Owl followed by the Victoria Hotel. Again, I kept walking. I had decided to find somewhere right in the village. When I could walk no further, I found The Bay Hotel perched at the very edge of the shoreline. I stood where the road ended and the sea began, and I thought: 'Yes, this is perfect.'

I booked in. I then climbed back out of the village to collect my car. I drove slowly down the hill and into the hotel's private car park. There was room for only three vehicles. My parking skills are minimal. Luckily trade was slow.

I wasn't sure how long it would take in Whitburn, so I decided to book into a local hotel. I asked for advice at the Bay Hotel's reception, and they recommended the Roker Hotel, Seaburn. I phoned the hotel to book a room.

I had a long hot bath and then I slept for a few hours. I had an evening meal at the Boathouse Bistro across the road from The Bay Hotel. I had grilled lemon sole. I was told it was caught locally. I washed it down with a bottle of very cold Pinot Grigio. After the meal I walked up the cobbled pathway up Covet Hill and down the wooden steps to the concrete Sea Wall Promenade. I sat on the bench and watched and listened to the North Sea crash on the rocks below. It wasn't long before the clouds began to form into a woman's face.

I returned to the village and found a warm pub. Blackburn's defeat at Coventry meant that United had secured their second successive championship victory. This gave me every excuse to get drunk. I had a quick phone conversation with Andi and then I started to celebrate.

I went to bed drunk and dreamed I was swimming with mermaids wearing Man U tops in the sea off the coast at

Staithes. Mrs Morney was leading the u-n-i-t-e-d chant.

I got up early and repacked my small black suitcase. I checked my AA map. It was straightforward. I had to get back to the A19. I would then stay on this road until very near Sunderland, leaving at the third sign for the city.

It was about 9.30 when I set off for Whitburn.

The journey was uneventful. The traffic was light. I spent most of the time wondering whether I was wasting my time going to see Mr Morney. I wasn't even sure what I would ask him. What made things worse was that I knew that deep down inside I almost believed that I would find Rebecca Morney there. Delusional thinking is not good for detective work. Rebecca Morney being there was possible, I suppose, but very unlikely. Very, very unlikely, given everything I had been told by Mrs Morney.

I stopped for brunch at a Happy Eater on the A19. I had scrambled eggs on toast and two cups of coffee. I arrived at the Roker Hotel at 12.18. The receptionist was very friendly, almost to the point of being intrusive. She asked questions about where I was from, why I was here, had I been here before, and lots of other things about my personal life. I answered politely but without being very forthcoming. She seemed not to mind. She smiled at everything I said.

'You are early. We don't usually check people in until 2 o'clock. But because it's such a lovely day, I will make an exception for you. By the way, my name is Liane. If you need anything, just let me know.'

I thanked her and I was shown to a room overlooking the sea. The beach was quite busy, mostly people walking with dogs. The North Sea looked cold and unwelcoming. It confirmed what I already knew from Whitby, I would not be going swimming. Then an involuntary thought: I could have sailed from where I stood last night to where I stand now. Perhaps in the past this is how it would have been done?

I unpacked my small black suitcase again. I went into the

bathroom and rinsed my face with cold water. I then returned to the reception area; a very large old man had replaced the nosey young woman.

'Hi,' I said.

'Hello. Can I help you?' His totally bald head shone under the gleam of the bright hotel lights.

'Can you tell me how to get to Whitburn?'

'Yes, it's very straightforward. Basically, you turn left out of the car park, follow the road along the coast and you will be there in about seven minutes.'

I thanked him and looked in my pocket for Mr Morney's address.

'Are you going to look where Frederika Liddell lived?'

I must have looked puzzled, so he explained. 'She was the cousin of Alice Liddell. You know, Alice Liddell, the supposed model for Alice in *Alice in Wonderland*. Have you read Lewis Carroll's books?'

I told him I had read Alice in Wonderland and *Alice Through the Looking Glass* as a child, but that was not why I was here. He seemed a little disappointed. Disappointed or not, he was determined to say what he wanted to say. He stepped from around the counter, held me by the arm and gently turned me around to face the door leading out to the beach. He had very dark blue eyes.

'Carroll spent a lot of time here. He met Frederika on the beach outside. Some people at the university believe that she is the real model for Alice. They even claim that you can map both books onto the local geography. One local historian has found the rabbit hole.' He was laughing now. The laughter was loud, rumbling from deep within his very large body. 'That part is a joke. It is not true. The rabbit hole, I mean. But the rest is true.'

I smiled and reached into an inside pocket in search of Mr Morney's address.

'Most people not from Sunderland think it is a backwater, a place on the periphery of things. But did you know it was once the largest ship-building town in the whole wide world? Can you believe that?'

I said, 'Wow, that's really impressive.' I also said that Sunderland seemed like a nice place to me. This was more than enough encouragement for the very large old man to continue.

His dark blue eyes sparkled, and his big bald head shone. 'Did you know that the first actor to be knighted made his stage debut here in Sunderland? Sir Henry Irving.'

Before I could respond, he was giving me a lecture.

'Ulysses S Grant, who won the American Civil War for the North and then became President of the whole USA, visited here. LS Lowry spent many summers here. We have some of his seascapes in our museum. Tony and Ridley Scott were born just down the road. You must like *Blade Runner*? Muhammad Ali was married a few miles down the coast. Do you like the Carry-On films? Sid James died on stage here. Jim Davidson died on stage here too. But he also died on stage in Newcastle, Durham, Darlington, Middlesbrough.'

The names of other places were lost in laughter, loud and rumbling laughter, making his large body tremble and shake.

'John Lilburne, the founder of the Levellers, was born here. Joseph Swan, the inventor of the light bulb, was also born here. Imagine what the world would be like without light bulbs; with so much darkness, what a terrible place. Without Mr Swan from Sunderland the world would be a much duller place. CW Alcock, the founder of the FA and the FA Cup, was born here.'

He was chuckling now. 'But best of all.' He paused for effect. 'Best of all, the Venerable Bede was born here. He worked here in the seventh century AD. Do you understand what that means?'

'You mean AD?'

'No, of course not. I mean that Sunderland is one of the oldest seats of learning in Europe. Forget Oxford and Cambridge, Sunderland is where it all begins.'

I pushed out my lips and nodded as enthusiastically as I could.

Although I was performing my enthusiasm, I was genuinely impressed, both by the information and by the large old man himself. No one was going to be allowed to think badly of Sunderland when he was around. He was a very effective one-man tourist board.

I finally found Mr Morney's address. 'Can you tell me how to get to this address?'

I handed him the piece of paper. He looked at it and then he read the address out loud, '30 Adolphus Street, Whitburn. It's right in the middle of the village. After you enter the village, take the first right after the second set of traffic lights and then the first left. Number 30 is about halfway down on your left-hand side. You have friends living there?'

I said yes, thanked him and started to leave. Just as I began to open the door, he shouted after me: 'On your left by the first set of traffic lights you will see what remains of where Frederika used to live.'

'Ok,' I said. 'Thank you for everything.'

'My pleasure, young man.'

The car park was now quite busy, which made reversing my car round and out a little difficult. I managed it, just. I turned left on to the coast road. The sea was coming in fast. The waves were high with white foamy tops. There was not much room left for walking, with or without a dog.

The large old man was right, I was in Whitburn in exactly seven minutes. I found the house easily. I parked the car a little beyond number 30 and did a quick mental recap of what I was going to say to Mr Morney. This involved me flicking rather pointlessly through my notebook. I was a little nervous, I guess.

The houses on both sides of the street were terraced. I was struck by their height. All were so very low. Although they clearly had rooms upstairs, these looked as if they had been added later, the houses themselves were not much higher than an average bungalow.

Number 30 had a bright red front door. It looked as if it had been recently painted.

I knocked on the door and waited. There was no answer, so I knocked again. Still there was no answer. I looked around. The street was empty. I looked towards the windows of the two houses on each side and directly opposite. There was no sign of life.

I reached into my pocket and pulled out a small penknife. Andi had bought it for me as a Christmas present. It was like the kind of knife a boy scout might carry with him on a camping trip. She had said that it would come in handy for those moments when illegal behaviour was the only means to bring retribution to the bad guys. This seemed like such a moment. I looked at the different blades and selected one I thought would do it. I looked around again. I was sure that I was not being watched. The small blade made very quick work of the lock. I stepped inside and closed the door. I was in a small corridor.

Ahead of me was a steep staircase, and on my left were two wooden doors. I opened the second door and entered what looked like the living room. The furniture looked very old and expensive. The room lead into the kitchen, and beyond this a bathroom. I did not see anything to interest me, so I left these rooms and entered the front room. As was the case in the living room, the furniture was old and expensive. Closing the door behind me, I climbed the steep stairs. The front bedroom was furnished in much the same manner as the two rooms downstairs. I entered the back bedroom.

The smell made me want to vomit. The room was very dark. I walked over to draw the curtains. I saw Mr Morney before I had had chance to let full daylight into the room. I opened the curtains fully to take a better look. The rope was fastened to a beam that ran diagonally from one corner of the room to the other. I covered my mouth with my handkerchief. The smell was getting worse. Mr Morney's face was like something out of a horror film. I could hardly look at it. But I saw enough to suggest that he had changed his mind when it was too late to do so. I looked away and noticed two bright white envelopes on the bedside table. On one envelope was written the single word Rebecca, and on the other the name of her mother. Both names were written in beautiful handwriting in thick black ink.

I closed the door and stumbled down the stairs. Outside, the air tasted fresh. I got in my car and drove back towards the hotel. I stopped the car next to a phone booth and phoned the police. They became irritated when I wouldn't give my name and address. I didn't argue, I just put down the phone. I got back in the car and drove to the beach near the hotel.

I walked for almost an hour on what the sea had left of the beach. The sea breeze gradually removed the taste from my mouth and the smell from my nostrils.

It was 1.37 when I got back to the hotel. I looked at my watch for a long time, wondering if I should just drive back to Manchester. My visit to Whitburn had proved to be a dead end. I said that again in my head and shuddered. I decided to drive back to Manchester.

Chapter Thirteen

Tuesday.

I woke up with a very bad hangover. I eventually got up at 11.08 and went into the bathroom. I looked awful. My face looked like it had been lived in roughly and the tenants had moved out. I filled the sink with cold water and rinsed my hands and face. I shaved, showered, and got dressed. Yellow shirt. Black shoes. Dark-blue suit. I looked and felt better.

The living room was exactly as I had left it the night before. I quickly tidied away a few things, mostly empty beer bottles, and turned on the radio to hear the weather forecast: bright and sunny all day. Fabulous.

I removed my jacket and prepared breakfast. I picked up two copies of *The Guardian* from the hallway floor. I propped Monday's copy against an empty vase on the breakfast table. I ate three pieces of brown toast, spread with honey, and drank two cups of Kenyan medium roast coffee.

SOUTH AFRICA "FREE AT LAST". At the bottom of the page, in much smaller print, under the headline, 'Soccer stylists top again,' I read the account of Blackburn's defeat.

The phone rang at 11.47. It was Sally Wilson.

'Hi. How are you?'

'I'm just fine, silly. What about you? Feeling better now?'

'I'm okay.'

'You've recovered, then?'

'Yes. I think so.'

'Anyway, I'm phoning to tell you that I've found Rebecca. Would you like me to take you there? She's in a house in Withington.'

'That's great. That's fantastic news, Sally. Yes, I would.'

'I'll pick you up from your apartment at about 12.30. I have a car now.'

'That's great. Okay, 12.30. I'll be waiting outside.'

'What is great, 12.30 or my car?'

'Both.'

'Tom, you can be very silly. I must go now. See you at 12.30. Bye.'

'Bye.'

I put the phone down and looked at my watch. I quickly cleared away my breakfast things, all the time thinking about what Sally had said. Would the case end so casually?

At 11.58 the phone rang again. It was Carol.

'We're running a story in the paper tonight that should be of interest to you.'

'Do I have to buy the Bolton Chronicle, or are you going to tell me now?'

'The old copper was right, it wasn't suicide.'

'Warner?'

'Come on, Tom, don't play the hardboiled detective with me. Yes, of course I am talking about Warner. How many other suicides have you been involved with recently? Warner was murdered. The police are in no doubt now. The forensic evidence is overwhelmingly convincing.'

'Thanks, Carol. I owe you a drink.'

'You owe me a whole brewery.'

'What if I buy tonight's Bolton Chronicle?'

'That should do it. Speak to you soon. Bye.'

'Bye.'

I didn't know what to think. Warner had been murdered. Rebecca Morney had visited his house with a man with a posh accent and a green sports car on the day of the murder. I had thought she might have pushed him over the edge, should I now think that her role was even more significant, even more central? No, that didn't make sense. But the man with her, the man with the green sports car and the posh voice, he had been seen arguing with Warner.

Sally arrived at 12.16. I invited her in while I put the final touches to my appearance. I brushed my teeth and put on my jacket. I was a little anxious about how our night together might interfere with her offer to help. But it was hardly a night together, I said to myself. Anyway, I had been tripping for most of it. I also felt a little guilty that I hadn't really been in contact with her since that night. But she was here, and she seemed to want to help. And she looked fantastic.

She was dressed in red trainers, tight blue jeans, and a baggy green sweater. Her hair was loosely tied back. There was something about her, as they say. She certainly exuded health. It didn't make me feel any better. Perhaps it would later?

'When he'd said you should buy some Pepcid, I suspected then what he'd done.'

She responded to my look of incomprehension. 'Pepcid AC is a brand of heartburn tablets. The phrase 'acid control' is written in big letters on the packet. This amuses Guy. He can be very childish like that. Every time the ad comes on TV he rolls around laughing. It's become a sort of code he uses to indicate when someone is tripping.'

'Especially when the person tripping does not know he's tripping?'

'Yes,' she said, smiling.

'He does this kind of thing often?'

She ignored my question and continued with her explanation. 'I hesitated because I didn't think that even Guy could be that stupid. I didn't think he was reckless enough to slip acid to someone he didn't know; didn't know what they were doing, where they were going. He's so unbelievably irresponsible.'

I locked the door and we walked to her car, a blue Citroen Diane. She unlocked the car door and let me in. She climbed in and smiled. I smiled back. Then I saw what was hanging from her rear-view mirror.

'That's not a good start,' I said, pointing at the small pale blue shirt hanging down.

'Someone has to support the local team.'

'Yeah, right.'

She was laughing as she started the engine and headed for Withington. She changed gear to take a left turn on to Wilmslow Road. The car gradually built-up speed again.

'We've asked him to find somewhere else to live.'

'Don't throw him out on my account.'

'It's not just this. There are other things.' She stopped and considered for a moment. She opened his mouth to say something but changed her mind.

'Are these other things connected in any way with Rebecca Morney? I mean, with her disappearance?'

'It's possible. I don't really know.'

'Sally, yes or no?'

'Well, what Polly said is only partly true. He and Rebecca did go out together. It didn't last very long, but there was a relationship. Rebecca ended it. Guy was upset, very upset. You know the kind of thing. He tried hard not to show it, but he was very hurt.'

I knew the situation all too well, but I didn't reply. She waited for me to say something. I waited for her to continue. My instinct, or at least my experience as a detective, told me there was more. Remaining silent might ease it out. Just wait, I said to myself.

'He wouldn't let it go. Wouldn't recognise it was over. He simply smoked more dope and talked and talked about how she would come to her senses. Realise the error of her ways. You know, that kind of thing. He just could not accept it was over. Rebecca was no longer interested. I'm not sure she really ever was.'

She turned right off Wilmslow Road into Carlton Avenue.

'It's not far now,' she said, smiling. I smiled back. 'I think Warner's death scared Rebecca,' she said, with no intention to elaborate.

I nodded, knowing she would only elaborate if I didn't press her too much.

'When did she last see Warner?'

'She has not seen him since she stopped attending lectures and seminars about a month ago.'

I knew this wasn't true, but I saw no point in saying as much. The question that bugged me was did Sally know it was not true?

After another brief pause she spoke again. 'Guy tries so hard to be a hippie.' She laughed. 'He reads all these books about the sixties. Goes on and on about how wonderful it was. But he just can't do it.'

'What do you mean?'

'He can't be the kind of person the books tell him he should be. When Rebecca told him she was seeing someone else, rather than launch into his usual dopey talk about free love, he exploded. Who? How long? Why? Some people just can't tell the difference between falling and flying. I told him he shouldn't confuse his fantasy with reality. He told me to leave philosophy to philosophers. He always says stuff like that whenever someone disagrees with him.'

'You should have quoted Gramsci at him. You know, we are all philosophers, etc.'

Her mouth curled into a big smile. 'Yes. But he probably had a point.'

I agreed but said nothing.

'She would not tell Guy the name of her new lover. All she would say was that he was a lecturer at the university. This was enough to make him explode again. She was a bitch. She was a whore. She was a tart. She was a fucking cunt. The language got more and more abusive. It didn't seem to matter that Polly and I were there in the room with them. He slammed about, kicking furniture, knocking things over, and yelling abuse at Rebecca. He would kill the bitch. He hit her. Once. Well, sort of slapped her face, quite hard. She responded with a pot Buddha, a very hard and determined blow. I was really surprised at her ferocity. Blood poured from his head. Together we managed to get him out of the house. He didn't come back for three days. He had been to the hospital. The white strapping around his head made no one doubt that he had. In the meantime, Rebecca moved out - to Withington.'

'But you let him come back? You let him continue to live there?'

'He was contrite, pitiful, really. He slobbered and made promises. We agreed he could stay until he found another place, or we found someone else. The truth was we needed his share of the rent. A case of economic reality forcing us to compromise our principles.'

'When did all this happen?'

'About four weeks ago.'

I gave a look of disbelieve. Sally responded: 'He's harmless enough, at least with us. Polly makes the odd comment now and then, like when you came around, just to make sure the fuse has been detached. His trick with the acid was not acceptable. But mostly he seems harmless.'

I would have to find out for myself. But I'd be careful.

Sally stopped the car at a red traffic light on Wilmslow Road. She turned to me and smiled. I said, 'What?' She said, 'Nothing, silly.' And kept smiling. She was still smiling when the car behind beeped its horn.

The house was a three-bedroom semi, the kind of house that is the mainstay of suburbia. Probably built just before the Second World War. It was the kind of house the BBC always present as a typical English family home. It was certainly not the sort of house students usually live in alone. Again, I saw the hand of the man Guy called Moneybags Morney, the man

I had seen hanging from a beam in a sad house in Whitburn. To block that image, I asked the obvious question.

'How does a student afford to live here alone?'

Sally smiled and lifted her eyebrows. That was her only answer. Lucky for her she did not have to struggle with the image of a man hanging from a beam.

But there was a bigger question. Did Rebecca Morney know about her father's death? If not, do I tell her? Or do I tell her to contact the police? Contact her mother? I had no idea what to do? I consoled myself that she probably knew already. But she couldn't know. If she knew, she would have surely told Sally.

We got out of the car. Sally retrieved a grey leather jacket from the boot. She put it on and immediately sunk her hands in to the deep pockets. She stood quite still, waiting, smiling. I said, 'Ok,' and she was animated again.

There was no response to my knock on the door. I stepped back. Nothing.

'You're sure she's here?'

'Positive.'

Sally pushed open the letterbox.

'Rebecca, it's me. Come on, Rebecca, open up.'

There was silence, then a shuffling sound.

'Go away. I don't want to speak to anyone.'

The voice surprised me. Not so much the anger and fear I thought I heard in it, but the grain of the voice. It was much deeper and more mature than I had imagined after looking at her photograph every day since Fish had first given it to me. Above all, she sounded very sad. Perhaps she did know about her father? Perhaps she had already spoken to her mother?

'But Rebecca, it's *me*. I've brought Tom Renfield the detective to see you. Remember, I told you about him?'

'Look, I don't want to see anyone, especially not him. Go away. Please take him away, Sally.'

Sally looked embarrassed, but also a little concerned. I eased her away from the letterbox. Her arm brushed firmly against my side. Rather than wonder whether her contact had been deliberate, I focused on my task. I could not see Rebecca Morney, but I knew she was standing behind the door. I waited, hoping she would move her body to where I could see it. I wanted to see her body move, the beautiful body I had seen frozen with the traffic in Fish's photograph. Why would someone like that want to sleep with Warner?

'Can we come in for a moment,' I said, with polite hesitation.

'Look, just leave me alone.' She said this without moving her body in to my line of vision. Before I could say another word, Pachelbel's *Canon in D* was playing at a deafening volume. Its big brushstrokes of sound seemed to be mocking me. The music had been played at my mother's funeral. It was a strange way to tell me not to speak anymore and to go away. But she couldn't possibly know the place of this music in my own unhappiness?

My train of thought was ended when Sally tugged at my sleeve. She held on longer than necessary.

'Tom, I'll come back later. I'll try to convince her to speak to you. It's obvious she won't now. Let's just go. Tom, let's just leave.'

I could see it was hopeless. I was more than a little irritated. It occurred to me that I could just phone Fish, tell him where she is and end the whole thing then and there. Instead, I said: 'Ok. Should we go to the pub or something?'

We walked back down Egerton Road. The Friendship is a large pub, popular with students. It was quite full for a Tuesday. I bought the drinks. I had a pint of Fosters, and she had a glass of diet coke. We found a table near the Wilmslow Road entrance. My irritation was draining away very quickly. It was beginning to feel like I was on a date. Stupid, I know.

On the wall in front of our table, Sally drew my attention to an old map of the area.

'Did you do history?'

'No, English.'

'You should have done history.'

I smiled.

'Too much, man. As Guy would say.'

'What?'

'I'm joking, silly.'

I loved the way she called me silly. For reasons I could not fully understand, it produced a chill that ran its fingers slowly down the back of my neck.

She asked what it was like being a private detective. Was it a tough job? Did I ever get hurt? I told her the story of how a tree had once saved me from a possible spell in hospital.

'I was once working on a case where I'd arranged to meet a witness in a public park after dark. Something told me to be wary, so I turned up an hour before the arranged time and climbed a tree and waited. He turned up thirty minutes early with two friends armed with baseball bats. The idea was to warn me off the case. I stayed quietly up the tree. They waited an hour and left. I reported the incident to the police. They laughed and told me to get a proper job. As Dylan said, 'the cops don't need you and, man, they expect the same.''

Sally smiled a knowing kind of smile. 'I love Dylan, but I'm not sure if I believe your story.'

I wanted to reach out and touch her arm. Before I could make a move, she said: 'I'll go back now. I'll see if I can convince Rebecca to talk to you.'

'Okay. I'll wait here for you. It's going to be tough work, but I think I can manage it. I'm joking, silly,' I added, wondering if it would produce the same effect on her. I couldn't tell. She got up, smiling and waving at me as the door closed behind her.

I bought another pint and waited for her to return. I was thinking how much I liked being with her when she returned. She was back much sooner than I had expected. I was not expecting what she would tell me.

'She's not there,' she said quietly, as if she was telling me a secret.

'Not there? What do you mean?' I was trying not to sound too angry.

'I mean, she's gone somewhere else,' she said, responding to the signs that I was angry.

'Are you sure?'

'Yes, I'm sure. I knocked and knocked without answer.'

I had made a stupid mistake. I should not have gone to the pub with Sally. I should have waited outside the house. I was allowing pleasure to get in the way of business. I was very annoyed with myself.

'Where would she go?' I said, trying not to allow the anger I felt to come between us.

'I don't really know. There are lots of places.'

'Yes. I'd guessed as much. But where do you think she's gone?'

'She might have gone to Whitby.'

'Whitby?'

'Yes. She has a house there. Well, it really belongs to her parents. You know, a sort of holiday home.'

'But her parents only live in Staithes?'

'Not that kind of holiday home, silly. They don't stay there. They let it out during the summer.'

I did not know what to believe. I tried to think. Was Sally helping again? Or was she helping her friend?

'She has gone to Whitby. I spoke to her before she left. I said I wouldn't tell you. But I can't see what harm there is in you talking to her.'

I didn't know how to respond. Should I be pleased that she was telling me? Or should I be angry that Sally had colluded in Rebecca's escape. Should I even believe what I was being told? But I quickly convinced myself that sometimes you must trust people. I so wanted to trust Sally. Irrational or not, I smiled and asked her to write down Rebecca's Whitby address.

She wrote down the address with a pencil on a scrap of paper she pulled from her jacket pocket. The handwriting flowed in all directions. I held the note as if it contained a promise of a better world. I turned it over. There were other notes. It was obvious that the notes were the first attempt at an essay plan. She watched me read it.

As if in response, she said: 'The plan is better now.' Adding, 'Have you ever read John Clare's poetry?'

'Yes, I have.'

'Those are some quick notes I made on how I intend to structure an essay on his wonderful asylum poems. I really like them.'

'So do I.' I was tempted to add that it was something we had in common, something that might survive the end of the Rebecca Morney case. Instead, I did not say anything. I just kept smiling, my right hand in my pocket, my left fiddling with my shirt collar.

First thing in the morning I would drive to Whitby again. I thought about that for a moment. No, I would go on Thursday morning. Wednesday evening, I had a 'business dinner' with Andi. It was an easy decision. What was harder was whether I should invite Sally.

I thanked Sally as she left, saying she had to be somewhere else. I wanted her to stay. For a moment I thought about following her. But I did not. I stayed in the pub and had another pint.

Once I was certain she had gone, I phoned Fish. 'I've located Rebecca. She's in W . . .' The W sound stuck in my throat. I tried to think quickly. 'She's in Withington.'

'Excellent news. You've done very well. First class, again. I mean it, Tom, first class work. I need to speak to her, make sure everything is okay. Will that be possible?'

'She's not answering the door just now, but I'm sure it will be okay.'

'Oh, I see. Well, I'll call around later. Or I'll phone. Or something. Let me get a pencil for the address.'

I gave him the Withington address, knowing that on Thursday I would drive to Whitby to talk to Rebecca Morney.

I had broken the private detective's code as preached by every detective - *the client comes first*. And I didn't know why.

I decided to have another drink.

Chapter Fourteen

Later the same day.

I was coming out of the Manchester Public Library when I quite literally bumped into Guy. I had been checking some phone numbers for Andi on my way to the office. Guy looked startled and more than a little anxious.

'Too much, man,' Guy said.

Before I could form a sentence in response, he turned and ran. Without really thinking about it, I pursued him.

He ran in to Peter Street and then left into South Mill Street, between the Theatre Royal and the Free Trade Hall.

At the corner a busker was playing 'A Hard Rain's A-Gonna Fall.' The line 'I met a young girl; she gave me a rainbow' followed me down Windmill Street.

The clock on the facade of the G-Mex Centre said 2.17. I felt like I was running in a race I was officially too old to enter. I was certainly puffing enough. The beer I'd consumed earlier did not help.

I'm getting too old for this shit, I said to myself, as I followed him left into Watson Street. I wasn't even sure why I was running after him. I knew it was crazy, but I couldn't stop myself.

We passed what used to be, and is still boldly labelled, the Great Northern Railway Company's Goods Warehouse. It is now a National Car Park. So much for the confident world of Victorian capitalism.

I followed him into Great Bridgewater Street East and then

left in to Deansgate. Dodging through the angry, noisy traffic and into the Castlefield Canal Basin, it occurred to me that he hadn't done much tourism in the area. If he had, he would have known that he was running in to a dead end. Knowing this was a great relief.

I struggled with him on the bank of the canal. I pulled him to the ground. We didn't exchange blows. Rather, we wrestled. Eventually I pinned him to the floor. He stopped struggling. 'Okay. What do you want?' he said, exhausted. I didn't really know what I wanted. An explanation about why he had spiked my drink, more information about his relationship with Rebecca Morney? Revenge?

I got up. He got up. We dusted ourselves down and walked together back to Deansgate. Once on Deansgate we crossed the road and went into The Crown on the corner of Trumpet Street. We both knew there were things we had to talk about. But we also knew that there would be no more chasing or fighting. Drinking and talking was all we would do, possibly all afternoon. Delaying my visit to Whitby was looking more and more like a brilliant piece of detective planning.

The pub was full, mostly with tourists on their way to or back from the Castlefield Heritage Park. Little bursts of conversation could be heard about the Roman origins of Manchester or the oldest railway station in the world. I ordered two pints of Boddington's. We found seats at a table near the window overlooking the comings and goings on Deansgate. We were lucky. A group were just leaving. A small boy was carrying a toy train. I smiled at him as we waited for them to leave. His expression remained unchanged as he poked the train in my direction. This was his answer. A good answer, I thought to myself. I wanted to say to him, 'oldest train station in the world.' Instead, I just kept smiling.

Searching for money, Guy placed a rather crumpled pamphlet on the table. It was called *Rain*. 'I thought you were studying

English?'

'I am,' he said, opening the pamphlet. 'I was given this in the library. I've not looked at it properly, but I think it's advertising an art exhibition somewhere.'

He handed it to me. I flicked through it. It was advertising an exhibition. Paintings with the theme of rain in Manchester. It started with some general information about rain. I read aloud the opening sentence; *Rain is liquid precipitation that makes human life possible*. We both laughed, a little uneasily.

At first Guy's conversation was very limited. I knew I would have to be patient. Our talk danced around the topic of Rebecca Morney. Her name kept coming up - mostly introduced by me - but only to disappear to the margins again. We talked about lots of things: the university; eating out in Rusholme; the music of the sixties; the certainty that United would do the double. Towards the end of his third pint, Guy became less conscious of his surroundings and his potential audience. I'd now secretly switched to non-alcoholic lager, but probably too late to make any significant difference.

I studied his appearance. He was wearing white tennis shoes, blue flared jeans and a lilac silk shirt that had a kind of tie-die pattern. I remembered what Sally had told me about his desire to be a hippy. His dress code made this desire very clear. But dressing the part wasn't the problem, or so I'd been told.

He began to ramble. 'I didn't need to be reminded how attractive she was. I often watched her being watched by other men. Our relationship was like a loaded gun. When she was in the mood she could be a real sex vampire. You know, love at first pint. It would be a massive understatement to say that after a few drinks she was sexually uninhibited. She was like a cat in heat. She was very much pay-as-you-go, if you know what I mean?'

I had no idea what he meant, so I just nodded and drank a mouthful of beer. It did not taste good at all. But I was a little surprised by the forced brutality of the description. Male heartbreak and insecurity had once again found its favourite form of articulation - misogyny and the double standard. I figured Guy had been hurt badly. All the tough talk was just a facade. Behind it was pain. But what I found puzzling was whether it was his ego or his heart that had been damaged. Perhaps it's always a complex mix of the two.

'A lot of it was bullshit. Performance stuff. I know that. One night she explained to us all about what she called her celebrity fuck list. She gave us a count down from number twenty to number one. Morse was on the TV. So, I asked her if he was close to being on her list. She replied, 'I would have to be very drunk.' Everyone laughed. But I could tell that she was really serious, really serious.'

Halfway through his fourth pint, he began to soften. 'I'm really sorry about the acid, man. Sally told me about your other problems. I'm sorry about that, too.'

'It's okay,' I said, wondering what he'd been told. I was puzzled. I couldn't remember telling Sally anything about what he called my 'other problems.'

'I don't know why I did it, really.' Then speaking slowly, he said: 'I suppose I was angry with the male establishment at the university. I saw you as their proxy, I suppose. I couldn't get them, so I got you. I'm sorry. Really sorry, man.'

I found the phrase male establishment rather cute. I didn't say so. Instead, I mumbled, 'Displacement.'

He didn't seem to hear. He paused for a moment, he then continued with more confidence. 'You swallowed about 500 milligrams. The standard dose in the sixties and early seventies was 250 milligrams. Today on the rave scene it's more like 125.'

He said all this as if he was presenting a seminar paper on a cultural studies programme. I had to fight back my irritation. He then said some things about San Francisco and St Ives. He mumbled something about Jefferson Airplane and Country Joe and the Fish. I realised I wasn't really listening. I was drifting on alcohol-fuelled automatic pilot waiting for the sound of the magic words, Rebecca Morney.

'I don't know why I gave you 500. I'm really sorry about that, man.'

I half-expected him to promise he would not do it again. Instead, he said: 'I suppose you want to know about Rebecca?'

I tried very hard not to seem too relieved, too enthusiastic. But I was listening now. 'Only if you want to tell me,' I said, trying very hard to be cool.

'Oh no.'

'What's wrong?'

'That song.'

The jukebox was playing 'I Wish It Would Rain.'

'She thought knowing about black music made her cool. It was all taken from Polly. She didn't want to be Polly, she just wanted everything that Polly had.'

He remained quiet. I could not be sure if he was listening to the song or lost in some thought about Rebecca.

'I know Sally's told you we had a relationship. She's also told you how it ended. Her version, anyway.'

'Tell me your version,' I said, encouragingly.

He finished his pint. 'Same again?'

'No, you're a student, I'm a full-time worker, I'll get them.'

He hesitated, a little confused.

'Look. You get them, I'll pay.'

I handed him a £5 note. He took it and walked to the bar. I watched him order the drinks. He returned and put two pints of Boddington's on the table and then without speaking walked over to the jukebox. It was a relief to be back on real beer.

'I love this song,' he said, waving his left arm in the direction of the jukebox. Soul Asylum's 'Runaway Train' provided a soundtrack to Guy's account of what he kept referring to as 'his relationship with Rebecca.' He continually stopped to sing along. His account was punctuated with words from the song.

'You hit her?'

'Sally told you?'

I nodded and swallowed a mouthful of beer.

'Sally didn't hear everything. She didn't hear the whole argument.'

He paused. He suddenly looked very timid and very young. He drank a big mouthful of beer, almost emptying the glass. I turned away from him, wishing I hadn't confronted him so head on. I was sure it was going to prove counterproductive. I turned away and surveyed the faces of the other drinkers.

Guy rambled superficially from one topic to another. Then he returned to what he had never really left. 'It's hard when you love someone who doesn't love you. I don't mean staring from afar. I mean when someone lets you in and then lets you down. They make promises they cannot keep. They make promises they never intended to keep. It really hurts, hurts in a way that 'hurts' does not describe. Do you know what I mean, man?'

I didn't answer his question, there was really no need to respond.

'When she couldn't sleep she would count the boyfriends who she had been unfaithful with.'

Again, I didn't answer. He stopped talking for a moment. He seemed to have run out of words. Then he took a deep breath and finally said what he really wanted to say. 'She told me she was HIV Positive. She told me she'd known this before she had slept with me. She also told me that she'd already decided to end our relationship. Our relationship was over before she slept with me. But she slept with me, anyway, knowing she was HIV Positive. I know I shouldn't have hit her. I didn't mean to. I loved her. I was in love with her, and she returned this with contempt and corruption. I told her I loved her. She told me to take a blood test. It was the only way I could hurt her. But I didn't plan it. I just reacted. It wasn't a display of power, as Sally and Polly probably think, it was a display of weakness. Rebecca knew this very well. She seemed to rejoice in my weakness. The pot Buddha was unnecessary, it was just for dramatic effect.'

He swallowed hard and continued, completely oblivious to his surroundings now, uncaring who might hear what he said. There were tears forming in his eyes. 'Telling me she was HIV Positive didn't mean anything. I hit her out of desperation. It meant a relationship. Perhaps it's difficult to understand. I don't know. But I loved her. She didn't love me. She rejected my love, but she couldn't reject the pain I inflicted. The pain connected us. People say we hurt the ones we love. I hurt her to make her love me. I know it doesn't make sense. Nothing does anymore. Sorry, I'm just talking nonsense now. I think I'm a little drunk.'

'Me too,' I said.

He thought for a moment. 'After I've taken the AIDS test, things might be different. I don't know.'

I wanted to ask him why he hadn't taken the test already. Instead, I wondered if I would have behaved any better.

We walked back together into the centre of town. As we stumbled along he asked me if I had read about Warner's murder. He told me that Warner had taught he and Rebecca. I said very little in response to his questions.

We parted company at Cross Street. I caught the 106 outside Boots and opposite the Royal Exchange Theatre. I paid my 48p and found a seat. I got off the bus at The Church Inn and walked back along Cambridge Street to my apartment. I needed to drink some water and lie down.

The phone was ringing as I entered my apartment. As I lifted it, the ringing stopped. I replaced the phone and removed my coat. The phone started ringing again. I lifted the receiver and said 'Hello.' It was Sally and we arranged to meet at 8.45 outside All Saints Park.

I stared into the park; melancholy trees shrouded in a damp murky darkness. My head filled with the glow of a coal fire, something I had not seen since childhood. The image flickered away very quickly. I was very cold. My umbrella had done little to protect me from the rain.

After a while it became obvious that she was not coming. I looked at my watch again. I felt very cold. The rain was even heavier now. I looked at my watch again. I looked across at the park and then up and down Oxford Street. There were few people around and none of them looked anything like Sally, so I crossed the street and walked, slowly at first, back towards the centre of the city. I then changed my mind and walked away from the city. I drifted along past St Mary's Hospital and then over Whitworth Park, past the curry houses of Rusholme and on into the back streets of Longsight, where I found a pub I'd never been in before. I drank Boddington's bitter until the pub closed. It was a small pub with very few other customers. Other than when I ordered drinks, I spoke to no one, and no one spoke to me. I walked home and went to bed. I'd walked about eight miles. Eight miles high, I laughed to myself, thinking about Guy. I slept better than I had done for a long time, a long dreamless sleep, uninterrupted until the sound of milk bottles clattering outside.

Chapter Fifteen

Wednesday.

I woke up early but remained in bed listening to the day beginning: the birds, the sound of children's voices, the build-up of traffic on the road below. I listen to it with great seriousness, as if listening to a piece of classical music. As I did, I couldn't help wondering why Sally had not turned up. I decided not to phone to find out why. Male pride? I wasn't sure.

After breakfast I walked to the office to clear up some paperwork and prepare for my second visit to Whitby. I just wasn't in the mood for work, but I forced myself and managed to get a few routine things out of the way. I spent a lot of time thinking about Rebecca Morney and looking at her photograph. I had looked at her photograph so often I felt that she was someone I knew. Delusional thinking is not a good thing for a detective, I thought.

I turned the photograph over in my fingers, thinking that behind her beautiful eyes there must be a clue. I was missing it, but if I looked long and hard enough, it would become clear. I was sure it was there in her eyes, perhaps written in a foreign language I had yet to learn. I put the photograph back in the envelope and placed it in the bottom drawer of the desk.

I sat there and tried to make a mental list of everything I now knew about the case. It wasn't working, so I removed a pad of paper from the drawer and started to draw up a list. It was a very short list. I screwed up the paper and threw it in the wastepaper bin. I glanced at my watch. 11.43. Before leaving for lunch, I walked around the room thinking things over. Another unsuccessful attempt at a list.

I walked to the Sawyer's Arms on Deansgate. I liked the sandwiches they made. Everywhere claimed their sandwiches were fresh, but those seemed to be genuinely fresh. The pub was surprisingly empty. I decided to sit at the bar.

I had finished a roast chicken, butternut squash and chutney pickle sandwich on brown crusty bread and was just starting my second pint when a woman approached me and said, 'Are you Tom Renfield?'

I said I was, and she sat down next to me. 'We were at university together. You don't remember me, do you?'

I looked at her, smiled and said: 'Molly?'

She smiled and nodded. 'Yes. Would you like another drink?'

'Let me get them,' I said.

She laughed. She had the kind of laugh that made one feel at home. I ordered her a large glass of Pinot Grigio and myself another pint of Boddington's. She asked what I did for a living. I told her and she told me that she was working for a lifestyle magazine. We exchanged details of our respective jobs. Molly bought another round of drinks. We decided to sit at a table near the window.

She was small and slim, with short dark hair. Her skin was very tanned. She was wearing tennis shoes, blue jeans, a white cotton shirt and a blue denim jacket. I had hardly known her at university. But here we were getting drunk and pretending we were long lost friends.

Her accent told me she was from Liverpool, so I asked if she had returned home after she graduated from university. She told me that other than family visits, she had never left Manchester.

We both bought further rounds of drinks. Eventually we got talking about the Rebecca Morney case. She was particularly interested because of the university connection. She asked what

it was like to get so close to violent death. I told her that it was
as difficult as she could ever imagine. She talked about John
Donne to understand what I was feeling. I wasn't convinced
that Donne was really very helpful, but I did not say so. We
then talked about other things we had read together as students.
I told her about my mother, and she told me about David. He
was the man she had been married to for more than five years.
It was now all over. She joked that she could have used my
services. The relationship had not ended well, accusations and
counteraccusations. She blamed him, but some of the things
she said made me wonder if it was really that straightforward. I
suppose it never is. We had more to drink. She asked me where
I lived. I told her and she replied that it was a good place to
live. She had lived nearby as a student. I said she could visit any
time. She suggested that there was no time like the present. We
decided to buy some wine and go to my apartment.

We had talked a lot about our time at university. We were
both careful to avoid the fact that back then we had hardly
known each other. We talked about Fish and other members
of staff. She said she had read about Warner. But mostly we
talked about Fish. I was careful not to say too much about Fish
in connection to the Rebecca Morney case.

In the taxi, she asked me if I had a suspect. I told her that I had
several, but that my number one suspect was Fish. She laughed
and said, 'Fish would always be my number one suspect.' We
both laughed. I told her she would not be alone. I didn't tell
her that the case wasn't as simple as identifying a suspect. If we
were paid for everything we end up investigating, we would be
very rich indeed.

'Do you have any clues?' she asked, suddenly.

I smiled in a way that was meant to say shut up.

'Do you get to beat people up?'

'No, I'm not the police.'

'I hope not,' she said, reaching out her hand to touch my

left thigh. I was still puzzled. I could hardly remember her. I thought I could remember her being there in the background, but I remembered little else.

'What are you thinking about, Tom?'

'I was thinking that you have fantastic breasts,' I said without thinking.

She remained silent, as if quietly listening to my thoughts. She then looked me straight in the eyes. There was a question on her lips. But she did not ask it. Instead, she said, 'Why is he a suspect?'

'Who?'

'Fish.'

I thought for a moment. 'The only reason is that I suspect him.'

'That might be a good reason. Then again, it may be as irrelevant as my own reasons for suspecting him.'

'Maybe. Suspecting people is my middle name.'

'Strange name. Do detectives have to be good at counting?'

'Counting?' I said, a little puzzled.

'Yes. Two and two equals four. That kind of thing.'

'Oh, I see. Yes we do. Two and two can equal four, but it can also mean twenty-two.'

'That's what I meant,' she said. 'There is so much more to being a detective than meets the eye.'

'The private eye?'

'Exactly.'

'That's more or less what Fish said.'

'Forget Fish.'

'I wish I could.'

'I will help you,' she said, as she linked my arm.

I paid the taxi, and we climbed the stairs. I put the wine in the freezer compartment of the fridge. I then opened two bottles of San Miguel. I put them on the table. She looked at the beer and then at me.

'Show me your apartment,' she said.

When we reached the bedroom she sat down on the edge of the bed and gestured for me to sit down beside her. As I did, she kissed me. We rolled backwards on to the bed. I had to stop myself from holding her too tightly. Under the covers I felt safe and wanted. We made love and fell asleep. It was raining when we awoke. I looked at my watch, it was a little after 5 o'clock.

She seemed a little embarrassed. She said she had to go. We exchanged telephone numbers without much conviction. I phoned her a taxi and she left. I didn't know where she had come from, and I didn't know where she was going. But I was glad that we had met. I didn't know if we would ever see each other again. I didn't even know if either of us really wanted that to happen.

I made coffee and showered. I then felt almost sober.

I had arranged to meet Andi at 6.30. She wasn't there on time, of course. I wasn't particularly bothered. It was what I always expected. I was on my second drink at the bar when Andi arrived. It was 6.47. She was smiling and apologetic. I smiled and said, 'No problem.'

'Sorry I'm late,' she said.

'You're always late.'

'It's not my fault, I had to go to Urmston.'

'Lucky you.'

'You know what it's like, it has a different time zone. When it's 5.30 in Manchester, it's the 1970s in Urmston.'

I had been looking through the menu, unable to decide whether to have pizza or spaghetti. The Handsome Sailor from Naples was an unpretentious Italian restaurant. It was situated in the shadow of the Cathedral, in the medieval part of Manchester. Andi and I ate here at least once a month. As usual, she thought I was too conservative in my choices, either pizza margarita or spaghetti Bolognese, always washed down with several bottles of Peroni beer.

Olympia showed us to a table near a window overlooking the

street. Oly was a tall woman from Athens. We had gotten to know her quite well. Although she was Greek, she pretended to be Italian. When she had been interviewed for the job, it was made very clear to her that when working she was Italian and not Greek. This was a strict instruction from the manager, a man from Madrid called Eduardo. As Oly had told us, she was glad to change her nationality. Being Italian was good for tips. Customers expected authenticity, so she did her best to provide it.

Andi flicked through the menu. I looked out of the window at the movement on the cobbled street outside. The street was pedestrian only. People sheltering under umbrellas were hurrying to the left and right. Wouldn't life have been simple if Rebecca Morney had just walked by, stopped outside the window, smiled, and come into the restaurant and explain everything to Andi and myself? I was also hoping to see Warner. As if my wish had partly come true, I saw Trelawny. He was arm-in-arm with a tall, well-dressed, blond woman. They were snuggled together beneath a dark red umbrella, walking slowly towards the lights of Deansgate. As if I was watching a film, they stopped in the frame of the window and kissed. It wasn't a long kiss, but a passionate kiss. Too passionate, I thought, for the woman to be his wife. But perhaps my work made me too cynical. What was clear was that the woman was not Rebecca Morney. She didn't even look like a student: too old and too sophisticated. But I could be wrong. Anyway, I didn't suppose it mattered.

Taking a mouthful of Italian beer, I listened to Maria Callas singing 'Casta Diva.' I knew little about opera, but I enjoyed the beautiful melodrama of it all. Callas' voice had the ability to transport me to a better place. I was drifting to that place when Andi put down her knife and fork, lifted her napkin to her lips and announced, 'I think I'm going to have Garlic Chicken. What about you, Tom? Pizza or spaghetti?' she said, smiling.

'I'm going to have Spaghetti Bolognese. Should we have wine or beer?'

'You're already drinking beer, so let's have more beer.'

Oly took our orders. We chatted with her briefly about her recent decision to go back to university. We asked if she would study in Manchester or somewhere else in the UK, or back in Greece. She said she was still unsure quite where, but it would be in England. She was thinking particularly about London. She had family there. We wished her luck.

When the food arrived, we ate quickly and silently. It tasted good. It always did at The Handsome Sailor From Naples.

Then we talked about the Rebecca Morney case. Andi looked at me and smiled. She pushed some hair behind her left ear. She thought for a moment and said, 'In my limited experience, difficult cases always get worse before they get better.'

'So, there isn't a thing to worry about?'

'I didn't say that.'

I turned to my right and asked Oly for two more beers. She returned quickly with two more bottles of Peroni. I lifted my bottle and said, 'Here's to being great detectives.' I suddenly felt self-consciously drunk, wondering if Andi and Oly recognised that I was.

Andi clinked her bottle against mine and said, 'Let's hope it happens.'

'And soon,' I said.

We drank the beer and ordered more, and then began to talk about Andi's current case. She had been asked by an old friend, who she had not seen for many years, to find out if his wife was being unfaithful. The friend had recently returned to Manchester after working in Nottingham for several years, where he had met his current wife. Andi had been reluctant to take the job. She knew from bitter experience that when asked to carry out such an investigation it almost always resulted in confirmation of adultery. Sometimes the relationship survived, but mostly it did not. She did not want to be the wicked messenger, being paid to bring an old friend the bad news that would change his life. With great reluctance she had agreed to take the case. Most of her day had been spent following her old friend's wife around the city centre and beyond.

In the morning there had been nothing to report. She had followed her to work, then to buy a sandwich, a bottle of diet coke and a newspaper, the Daily Mail. At lunchtime she had followed her and a group of her colleagues into the Square Albert. She watched them eat lunch together. Again, there was no sign of infidelity. After about an hour they all set off back to work. It was then that the situation changed. The wife said goodbye to her colleagues outside the large building in the banking area above Cross Street. The others went inside the building, while the wife walked back alone towards Albert Square and then back into the Square Albert.

Once back in the pub she was greeted by a man sitting alone at the bar. He had been there during the wife's lunch with colleagues. She kissed him on his left cheek. He ordered her a drink. They collected their drinks and moved to a table in the corner at the far side of the pub. Andi moved her position but could not get close enough to hear their conversation. After about ten minutes, wife and friend got up and left the pub. Andi watched them from the window as they walked together across Albert Square. They looked like any other couple that might be there to admire the architecture of the Town Hall. But they seemed oblivious to the fact that it was there. They talked and laughed and looked only at each other. The man now had his arm around the wife's shoulders. She had her arm around his waist. Andi quickly got her camera out and photographed the couple without them noticing. She then followed them down Cross Street.

They stopped at the bus stop for the 23 to Urmston. Andi waited until others had joined the queue and then she joined it. Waiting for the bus, she examined the unfaithful wife of her friend. She was small and slightly overweight. Her hair was cut short and dyed blue. She talked as if she hadn't a care in the world. Every couple of sentences was followed by laughter. Andi thought that her friend could do better. Much better. But there is no explaining the mathematics of taste. She knew now that her friend's suspicions were well founded. But she also knew she needed more evidence. She followed them on to the bus; the fact that they remained oblivious to everything around them made following them very easy. They got off the bus a few stops before Urmston railway station. Andi followed them to a block of flats. She photographed them entering together. She checked the image on her digital camera. The time and date stamp were working.

Three hours later they came out together. Again, Andi photographed them. She now had enough evidence to confirm her friend's suspicions. They walked to the bus stop, where he said goodbye. No doubt she was going home as if she were returning from work. Andi now had the awful job of telling her friend the bad news.

Andi reported all this with an increasing sign of unease. She had not yet told her friend. I told her that the sooner she did it, the better she would feel. She agreed.

'Manchester is more and more like Sodom and Gomorrah. I can't decide if it is Sodom or Gomorrah.'

'It's one place.'

'What?' I said. My voice seemed too loud.

'Sodom and Gomorrah are one place.'

'No, it is two places. In Genesis it says something like, Then God rained fire and brimstone on the cities of Sodom and Gomorrah. Cities, not city.'

'All that time at Sunday School has not been wasted.'

We were still laughing when we paid the bill. We left a large tip for Oly and then decided to have a drink in one of the new bars on Deansgate. The rain had stopped. This convinced Andi that she would phone her friend. She would offer a meeting tomorrow morning. If he insisted, and she knew he would, she would tell him on the phone the details of what she had found out. I pointed out that her friend would be at home with his wife.

She pulled a sad face in acknowledgement of what I was saying.

'He is not a violent man, very gentle in fact. The most he will do is leave.'

'It seems so unfair,' I said.

'It always is. But this is what happens if you marry someone from Nottingham.'

Andi sat down on a bench outside the cathedral. She was holding her new mobile phone. I stayed on the pavement, wishing I was making a call to Fish, bringing that case to a successful conclusion. As I waited, I could hear little bits of Andi's conversation. She was finding it a very difficult call to make.

'Let's go,' she said with forced cheerfulness. 'You must be dying of thirst.'

'How did he take it?'

'Quite well, I suppose. He kept saying that he knew it was happening. But the more he said it, the more I think he was wishing he had never asked me to investigate.'

'It's best he knows,' I said, unconvincingly.

The bar was quite full for a Wednesday evening. We bought drinks and found a table. I told her that I was worried that the case was spinning out of control. I was again travelling to Whitby, the next day, with little understanding of why I was really doing it. Warner was dead, murdered, and I still wasn't sure of the full significance of his place in the case. Fish worried me, but he was my client. Andi listened to my worries and complaints.

She listened and smiled, and then said, 'Look, Tom, you are getting it all out of proportion. Warner's murder may have nothing to do with the case. Rebecca Morney's disappearance may be totally unconnected. As for Fish, he may be unpleasant, but he is paying you to find a missing person. Going to Whitby, because you've been told Rebecca Morney is there, is standard practice in such a case. You are being paid to do a job you love, so just enjoy it, and stop worrying so much. It's the uninvited acid that has brought you down. Tom, this is a job you can do, just do it.'

It all made sense. We celebrated with another round of drinks, and then another round, and then another. The last thing I remember is singing along to the jukebox. 'One of Us Must Know' had never sounded so good. The words had never sounded so true.

I went to bed very drunk. My sleep was deep and dreamless.

Chapter Sixteen

Thursday morning.

The sound of birds woke me to the world outside. I drank two pints of cold water, and sat quietly listening to the city wake up around me. I drank coffee on the small balcony, looking through the light drizzle of a new day. Like the rain, everything seemed to be falling.

I pulled my small black suitcase from the top of the wardrobe. I am never sure what to pack for such short visits. I thought for a moment and then filled the case, as usual, with underwear, a shirt, and toiletries.

This would be my second trip to the North Yorkshire coast in less than a week. I began to plan it like a tourist. I made another cup of coffee and scrutinised the road map.

In the early nineteenth century it was said that the quickest way out of Manchester for someone of my social class was via a bottle of gin. Luckier than my ancestors, I considered the alternatives. I could head south, circling Manchester on the M63. Or I could go north, across the city, directly to the M62. I decided on the latter. There is something appealing in driving through the quiet streets of Manchester on an early Thursday morning.

I put down my 1991 edition of the AA Road Atlas of Great Britain and made yet another mental note to myself to buy the 1993 edition. The 1994 edition might even be a possibility. You never know.

The early part of the route was straightforward. Take the M62, then the A1. Running my right index finger along the

A1, I considered whether to take the A64, circle around York, follow the road to Scarborough and then take the A171, which runs parallel with the North Sea, to Whitby. This would be the quickest route. However, I decided to privilege the prospect of scenery over the convenience of speed. I would take the A168, then on to the A170, thus skirting the North Yorkshire Moors National Park. At Pickering I would take the A169, crossing the moors between the two clusters of the North Riding Forest Park. Finally, I would enter Whitby on the A171.

It felt like I was planning a holiday. Andi should come. We could stay overnight. Go for a walk on the beach. But the Johnson case - another case of sexual betrayal - ruled Andi out. I'd decided not to invite Sally. I don't really know why. Well, I did know why: she hadn't turned up to our meeting at All Saints Park. But I also worried that I was again blurring the dividing line between business and pleasure. The confusion stemmed from the fact that, with Sally, I didn't really know where the dividing line began and ended.

I left the apartment at 6.45. Birds were still singing. The sun was struggling to break free of the clouds. A milkman was making his deliveries. A papergirl stood near my car, reading a newspaper she would shortly deliver. I smiled at her as I opened the car door. She didn't return my smile. Guiltily, she folded the paper and walked away. I smiled, remembering my own days as a paperboy. I enjoyed the work. Charging around on my bike and delivering newspapers didn't seem like work at all.

As I got in the car, sunlight suddenly burst through the clouds like righteousness leaking out of the doors of Heaven. It must be an omen, I thought.

The roads were as quiet as I had expected them to be. It wasn't until approaching Leeds that the traffic began to build up. Then I encountered very heavy traffic, lots of lorries and vans, moving slowly. I kept seeing Leeds supporters everywhere I looked. That must be a bad omen.

About thirty miles beyond Leeds, I drove off the A1 on to the A168. It was a beautiful spring morning. I noticed this for the first time. Ahead the North Yorkshire Moors dozed blue in the distance. Above the hills there was a white line in the pale blue sky. A child's line: boldly thick and murky white. Beneath it there was an old stone church. I found myself wondering who might visit there, who might pray to God in this old stone building. It reminded me of the church that lay at the centre of my childhood. But this church was more beautiful, sitting so far away from the urban clutter of a city.

I drove for a further two miles or so and then stopped at a Happy Eater. The time was now 8.30. The Happy Eater was like all the others in which I had eaten. Less people, perhaps. I ordered a toasted teacake and a large cup of coffee. Drinking my second cup of coffee, I tested my eyesight on the *Music On The Move* selection. I strained to read the titles: Bob Marley; The Shadows; Tina Turner; James Brown; Elvis Presley. I concluded the test on a CD called Movie (there was more but it was hidden from view). Satisfied, I paid my bill and left.

By following the signs for Castle Howard and Flamingo Land, I reached the A170 at Thirsk. I was now heading straight into the North York Moors. They seemed to rise and form a wall threatening to halt my progress. Rebecca Morney crept back into my thoughts. She was, hopefully, on the other side of the wall. Was it protecting her or imprisoning her? Which was she most in need of? Was she hiding or had she been hidden? Hopefully, I would know soon.

Ahead a police notice said that the road was unsuitable for caravans and heavy loads. My Volkswagen Polo was fine. I wasn't so confident about my head. It was full to overflowing with the Fish case. Or was it the Morney case? Being unable to properly name the case only made matters worse.

Approaching Sutton Bank signs reminded motorists to keep in low gear. About halfway up, I tried to shift from second to first and found third; the engine groaned its disapproval, the wheels skidded. I quickly found first. As I began to pick up speed again I waved in apology to the driver behind. She waved back. It was indeed a very beautiful spring morning.

After Sutton Bank the road quietly emptied. Most of the traffic had turned off at the information centre, probably to unload for a walk on the moors. The scenery was becoming more and more the material from which holidays are made. But I found it difficult to let go of dark thoughts of Rebecca Morney. Why had she gone to Whitby? What was so bad that she was hiding herself in this way?

I stopped for petrol at an Esso station just south of Helmsley. On the eastern edge of the town, I picked up two hitchhikers. They were heading for Whitby too. Their interest, or at least the interest of the young woman (the young man hardly opened his mouth throughout the journey), was *Dracula*. When she announced this I gave an involuntary smirk.

'I'm not one of those vampire nuts, you know,' she responded, with half-laughter. Pretending offence, she continued: 'I'm researching a PhD on vampires in nineteenth-century fiction. Bram Stoker's *Dracula* is a key text. You do know that part of the novel is set in Whitby?'

Yes, I did know.

Briefly, I thought of Warner. He might have been interested in her PhD. He might have been interested in her. He might even have been tempted again. Pale skin. Long, auburn hair, cut with a high fringe. Round gold-framed spectacles. Long legs. Short skirt. Much the same body shape as Rebecca Morney's in the photograph I examined daily. But I knew I was being unfair to him. We shouldn't speak ill of the dead, as my mother would have said. But what about historical research, as I learned to respond.

My new companions had set out from Birmingham the day before, stopping overnight at a friend's house in Wetherby. I was their second lift of the day. A woman selling farming equipment had taken them the forty or so miles from Wetherby to Helmsley. Two lifts from Wetherby to Whitby was quite good for a bright morning in early May, I was informed by the distracted and very reticent young man. Birmingham to Wetherby had taken nine lifts and all day. They were hopeful of keeping it well within single figures for the return journey. I wished them good luck. The young woman smiled. The young man continued to stare out of the window.

It was 9.45 when we reached Pickering. I turned left on to the A169. A sign read: Whitby 21 Miles. In less than an hour I might have some sense of why Rebecca Morney was hiding. The traffic thickened a little when we reached the high moorland.

'What's that?' the young woman asked, as we passed what looked like an enormous speaker.

'It belongs to RAF Fylingdales,' I said, suddenly unsure of how I knew this.

The young man then said slowly, his voice rising with every word, 'I'd like to hear The Orb through that system.' He was almost shouting by the end of the sentence. He then closed his eyes and placed his hands behind his head. After a moment or two he opened his eyes and lowered his hands, and returned to silently staring out of the window.

As if in response to the young man's movements, the young woman smiled in my direction. I smiled back and then I let my eyes wander a little over the moorland. Even in springtime it is a very bleak place, little more than rocks, heather, and small communities of sheep. Then my eyes caught the sea. It produced a funny half-remembered sensation, followed by a more focused memory of seeing the tower (or was it a windmill?) on the way to Blackpool, or the roller-coaster ride on the way to Ryhl. I could almost see my mother, camera in hand, thinking of photographs that could be taken. From behind a Box Brownie camera, she imagined the world that would come to define my childhood. Memories stored on four-by-four card.

I was beginning to order my memories when the young woman suddenly exclaimed, 'The abbey! The abbey!'

We all looked in the direction of the abbey. The young woman began to explain its significance. 'Just below the abbey is St Mary's graveyard. This was Dracula's first home in England. He came ashore as a large black dog and lived in the grave of a suicide. Mina first saw him there, as he drank the blood of Lucy. It's so exciting to be here at last. It really is. At last, I'm here. Fantastic. Fantastic.' As she spoke her glasses slowly slipped down her nose.

She talked and talked about the novel. It seemed as if the closer we got to the town, the more she had to say. It wasn't just a horror story. Imperialism, the New Woman, the unconscious, desire, sexuality, and so much more, were all to be found in this wonderful book. She talked about her research, about how she was going to make more than an original contribution to knowledge. She was going to change forever how people thought about the gothic novel. And central to her thesis would be her argument about how Dracula, the ultimate vampire, articulated the bourgeois fears and anxieties of late nineteenth-century England.

The final run in to Whitby was along the A171. Arriving motorists were greeted by a sign that read: WHITBY WELCOMES CAREFUL DRIVERS. I felt happy with that. I followed the signs for the town centre and parked the car in the long stay car park on the south bank of the River Eske. The time was 11.21.

I left the young man and the young woman at the Tourist Information Office. She was still talking about her PhD thesis when I said goodbye and made my way along the path around the harbour. My plan was to find Rebecca Morney and then to return to Manchester, with or without her. If it looked like taking longer than I expected, I would book into a hotel and return to Manchester the next day. I had left my small black suitcase in the car, hoping that it would not be needed.

As I approached the drawbridge across the river, I noticed a sign for the Dracula Experience. I smiled and thought of the young woman's PhD research. 'What was her friend on?' I thought to myself, smiling, as I crossed the bridge and examined the menu in the window of The Dolphin. It was too early for lunch, so I decided to check Rebecca's address first.

I crossed the road and made my way down Sandgate, a very narrow cobbled street, filled on both sides with small shops catering almost entirely for the tourist trade. I turned right at Market Square, then left along Church Street, a street very similar to Sandgate only wider. At the bottom of the street, on the left, just before the church stairs leading up to St Mary's Church, I walked into Henrietta Street. The air smelt of raw fish. Although I love fish, I hate the smell of it uncooked.

The street was cobbled and narrow, like Church Street and Sandgate. But there the similarity ends. Henrietta Street has only one shop, about midway down on the right-hand side, selling fish, lots of uncooked fish. My first impression was that the street looked like something from a television version of a Victorian novel. No doubt Warner would have disapproved. He would have looked at the street and felt disappointment bordering on outrage. He may even have formulated a footnote to be included in a refereed journal article. I didn't like the way I was beginning to sound like Fish.

Now I knew where it was, I would find Rebecca Morney later. I made my way back to The Dolphin. I ordered a crab salad and a pint of Flowers. The waitress made a joke about wakeful nights and dreams of vampires. When I asked her to explain, she recounted the tale of how Bram Stoker had supposedly dreamed the whole plot of Dracula after eating a crab supper during a stay in Whitby. Better to dream of vampires than some things, I thought.

The waitress was small, five-two, with short dark hair, cut in a bob. She had very blue eyes. We made eye contact a few times as she served other customers. We even exchanged smiles. There was clearly a mutual attraction. When she had finished serving, she took her lunch break at my table. Her name was

Gemma. She said she thought the story about Stoker's dream was probably untrue. She then told me she was not from Whitby. She had only lived here for about a year. Like the hitchhiker, the town's associations with Dracula had attracted her. She'd arrived with a boyfriend. He'd now gone back to Glasgow. He only stayed a couple of weeks. She was not sure why. I listened to her without making much of a contribution myself. She was a very confident woman. Eventually she asked if we could meet later for a drink. I said yes, unsure if I really wanted to spend another night in Whitby.

I returned to Henrietta Street and quickly located Hodge Cottage. It was a small town house situated above Tate Hill Pier. I recalled the words of the young woman: 'Tate Hill Pier was the spot where Dracula, disguised as a large black dog, first stepped ashore in England.' I looked back and up the steps leading up to St Mary's Church and the Abbey. The sunshine limited the flow of my imagination.

I knocked politely. There was no answer. I knocked again. I stepped back across the narrow street to watch for movement in the upstairs room. I waited a few moments. There was a slight quiver of the upstairs curtain. She was obviously home. I knocked again, but still no answer.

Trying to make myself as visible as possible, I backed myself slowly across the street. I waited a few minutes to make certain that I was being observed. Then slowly, with a rather hammy show of disappointment, I strolled back down the narrow street in the general direction of the bridge.

I didn't cross the river. Instead, I doubled back, through Market Square, along Sandgate and back on to Church Street, and cautiously back into Henrietta Street. I was careful this time not to be seen by anyone observing from Hodge Cottage. I found a passageway that allowed me to get behind the house. I was startled by the view. I was standing facing the mouth of the harbour. Below me was a small beach. I thought again of the young woman's description of Dracula's arrival in Whitby. I climbed on to the wall and into the backyard. The kitchen window was slightly open. I gently opened it wide. With little of the grace of a vampire, and without waiting to be invited, I entered the house.

What next? Did I secretly search? Or did I announce myself openly to Rebecca Morney? I was still undecided when I felt a very painful thud. The kitchen floor rushed up malevolently into my face. I was floating in a hard, garlic-filled darkness. I lost consciousness.

Chapter Seventeen

I awoke from a terrifying dream. Rainwater leaking into a cheap casket. I had been buried alive.

I was in a cold and dark place. I was frightened like a child. I was trying to reach out for warmth and safety when I awoke. I was in a very small and claustrophobic cellar. I could hear my own breathing growing louder and louder. My breathing was too rapid. I thought about the North Yorkshire Moors. I thought about the beach in Whitby and the North Sea. I tried to imagine myself as a bird flying in a big blue sky. I thought about Andi holding my hand. My breathing slowed down. I was almost in control again.

I was very cold and more than a little confused. I blinked my eyes to adjust to the darkness. My head really hurt. I could taste blood in my mouth. I did a quick tooth check with my tongue. All present and correct, more or less.

My face was pressed hard against a cold stone floor. My mouth tasted of blood mingled with dust. As my eyes focused slowly, I could feel a thumping pain in the back of my head. I tried to reach for the source of the pain, but my arms were tied tightly behind my back. I looked down. My feet were also tied. I was dazed and confused. I knew I must not allow my imagination to fill in the details of the darkness.

I had to think clearly. There must be a solution to this problem. Then I heard a faint noise, the small movement of dead flowers. I listened hard. Silence. I twisted my head towards the dead flowers. There was something moving underneath. A rat? I tried to get up. It was hopeless. The best I could do was roll a little. A little voice inside my head said do not panic. Another voice, much louder, reminded me of something I had once read about rats. The details were vague. I wasn't even sure if it was about rats in this country. There was a little hope in that thought. But I couldn't stop the trickle of information. Rat piss works like an anaesthetic. They piss on you while you are asleep. Your body becomes a feast, and you don't feel a thing. It is only when you wake that you feel and see what they have done. I shuddered, involuntarily.

There were other voices now. Other possibilities. Why had I been hit? But more than this, why had I been tied up and left in a cold dark cellar? Had I stumbled by accident into the den of the killer, Warner's killer? But why wasn't I dead already? Was there something more, something even worse than death, a terrible prelude to death? I didn't want to die like this, unprepared, alone in a cold dark place. I did not want these thoughts and this place to be the conclusion to my life. It seemed so unfair. I wanted to scream.

I needed to stop these thoughts and focus on escape. I knew they would only disable action. I needed to act. But first I needed to think straight. How long had I been unconscious? I had entered the house, and someone had hit me so hard I had been knocked out. But was that ten minutes ago or ten hours ago?. The way I was bound suggested that I had been here for at least an hour or so.

Fear gave way to anger. It grew in me like a football being inflated. It rapidly became hard and kickable. Who had done this to me? How dare they treat me in this way. I would kill the bastard. This couldn't be Rebecca Morney? God, if it was Rebecca Morney, perhaps I would only live as long as it took for her to know she was a suspect for Warner's murder.

I lay there for hours, cold and scared. Suddenly a door opened, and the frame was filled by a large figure. No one spoke. I looked at the large figure, the large figure looked at me, the silent staring seemed to last a very long time.

I could hear Vaughan Williams' *The Lark Ascending* playing on a radio in another room. The violin eased its way into what had become a tediously repetitive thud inside my head. The pain lessened. I closed my eyes, trying hard to transport myself back to the open meadow near my mother's house. I was almost lying on my back in the sunshine, surrounded by the welcoming yellow of buttercups, reading the shapes of the clouds, when a voice broke in. The large figure spoke, his voice sounding like that of a naval captain in a Second World War film: 'I thought you would never wake. You've been sleeping like a fucking baby. Academics are so fucking soft.' The swearing seemed a little forced, not part of his usual vocabulary. 'You're from the fucking university, right?'

I tried to play it cool. 'What about: "How are you?"' I asked with as much bravado as I could muster.

'Just answer the fucking question,' the voice responded without sympathy.

I thought quickly about how best to answer. I'm a burglar? I'm a private detective? I'm a vampire? I'm from the university? The last seemed the least challenging.

'Yes. I'm from the university. Rebecca's university,' I added, hopefully. But did he even know Rebecca?

'I know you are. I know who you are. I know what you are. I know what you want.' The words came out as a mechanical and menacing rattle.

Fear brought out bravado. 'You know a great deal. Tell me something.'

The large figure came forward from the shadows. How I wanted it to be Rebecca Morney. From the large figure came a hard kick. Under the weight of the first blow my body became one with the hard cold floor. Before the second, I experienced an overwhelming desire to sleep, to curl into a foetal position and slowly drift away, far away from the pain, into a soft welcoming light. I was letting go, drifting without pain. When the second blow landed it sent me spinning uncontrollably into a hard and uncomfortable darkness. For a brief moment I was safe in one of my mother's holiday photographs.

When I had first awoken, I had noticed, before the cold and the taste in my mouth and the pain in my body, a suffocating smell of rotting flowers. I turned my head and squinted my eyes. In the corner, piled in two heaps, were Lesser Celandines and Wood Anemones. Why? Should I ask? It didn't seem the most pressing inquiry, so I let it pass. Then again it might lighten the atmosphere.

Before I had time to formulate the question, the large figure in the shadows blistered my ears with an unprovoked attack on academic life. Instead of university, he had travelled to Australia. Every week he had written to Rebecca, telling her that academic life was a con, an obvious waste of time. She should get out and join him somewhere. But she was already too duped to leave. She had been sucked in and every day she was being sucked in a little bit more. The real Rebecca was being suffocated, transformed. She was imprisoned in a cocoon. But she would not emerge as a butterfly, but as a wingless beetle, doomed to scuttle here and there with no purpose or point. The more I heard, the more I wished he'd stayed in Australia. I started to laugh. I tried to stop myself laughing. I expected more violence but, thankfully, he was too self-absorbed to kick me again.

'She wouldn't be in this mess if she'd listen to me.'

I stopped laughing and I thought of Staithes. Did he know anything about Mr Morney and the lady of the office floor and the motel at the edge of some Midland town? Whatever he knew, I now knew for certain that it had been a mistake connecting myself with the university. But I didn't feel scared anymore. There was no need for further forced bravado. I was confident now. All his swearing and aggression was undermined by his ridiculously posh voice.

'I'm a private detective. I just want to speak to Rebecca Morney. I've been hired to find her. Is she here?'

I remembered her mother's insistence. 'Mrs Morney hired me to find her daughter.'

There was silence. The large figure was thinking about the changed situation.

'Do you have any proof of who you say you are?'

'In my inside pocket you'll find an identity card. There is also a blank cheque sign by Rebecca's mother,' I added, suddenly glad that I had accepted it.

The large figure came forward and reached a large hand in to my inside pocket. I got my best view of him yet, but perhaps not enough to pick him out in an identity parade. He had the build of a professional rugby player. I'd need a better description if I were ever to successfully press charges for assault and unlawful imprisonment. But I knew who he was. The blond hair and posh voice shouted out his identity.

The large figure held my identity card between his left thumb and his index finger. He looked with contempt at the small, laminated card with its passport photograph and brief text. Anyone could have one made, Andi and I knew that, but we still feel carrying it gives what we do a certain legitimacy. I suppose it makes us feel authorised. But we both knew that we should invest in better cards. As she said on a fairly regular basis, better cards might mean better business. We would have to see. It was something else we might spend the money on from the sale of my mother's house.

He read the information on the card. It was brief and to the point. At the top: **AndTom Detective Agency**. This was followed by an address and a telephone number. At the bottom: **Proprietors Andi Hunter & Tom Renfield**. He didn't find the cheque. I'd left it back in Manchester.

'Do you have a driving licence?'

'In the other inside pocket.'

The large figure leaned forward again out of the darkness and reached into my other inside pocket. This time I worked hard on a description: a large man, with the build of a professional rugby player, early twenties, wearing expensive aftershave, but still not enough to press charges and make them stick. But he was definitely the man with the sports car.

He read the details on my driving license.

'Where's the fucking cheque?'

'It must be back in Manchester. Look, if you're such a good friend of Rebecca's, phone her mother and she will confirm my story.'

This seemed to calm him down. 'Ok,' he said. 'So, you're a private detective looking for Rebecca. Why?'

'Why am I a private detective, or why am I looking for Rebecca?'

Conversation with the large figure was bringing out the worst in me. But for reasons I didn't quite understand, I seemed determined to bring the worst out in him.

'Don't get fucking smart. I'm Rebecca's oldest friend. I'm just protecting her.'

I sensed a definite change of attitude. The large figure no longer seemed absolutely savage. He almost seemed human. Suddenly the light went on. The light burnt into my eyes. I blinked and squinted. Gradually my vision cleared, and I could focus again. It had taken me a few moments to adjust my eyes to the light. But I now knew for certain that the large figure was human. He no longer even looked like a professional rugby player. More like the build of a tall athlete. A sprinter. Much less threatening. He was wearing a very expensive sweater, brown cords, and brown brogues. He looked like the kind of person who could recite the names of all the kings and queens of England. His blood probably ran red, white, and blue.

'My name's Mike Connor.'

Unthinkingly, he stuck out his right hand to shake hands. I smiled. Connor smiled back. I hoped this meant no more rough stuff.

He had blue eyes and blond curly hair. He was the man who had gone to Warner's with Rebecca. He was the man who had argued with Warner. But had he done more than this? Had he gone back later to continue the argument? Perhaps I was wrong to feel so confident that I was safe now?

'I'm her oldest friend. She tells me everything. But she's not here. Honestly, she's still in Manchester.'

'How do you know?'

'I was on the phone to her just before you arrived.'

'Can we talk somewhere else? The smell of the flowers makes it difficult to concentrate. Being tied up like a Christmas turkey also makes it difficult.'

He nodded without saying anything about the flowers or the fact that I was tied up, badly bruised, lying on a cold cellar floor.

I was trying to think quickly. Was this the man Guy had talked about visiting Rebecca in her first term at Manchester? If he was, did it really matter? But more importantly, and more frightening, did he have anything to do with Warner's murder?

'I thought you were him,' he explained.

Before I could ask who he thought I was, he asked, very politely, 'If I untie you, will you accept my apologies and let bygones be bygones?'

'If I say no, you won't untie me.'

'Look, I told you I am sorry. I made a genuine mistake. We are both on the same side, on Rebecca's side.'

I had no idea whose side I was on, but I knew I did not want to spend another moment on the cold cellar floor. There was also the possibility that he might be Warner's killer. If that was the case, being tied up was not a great position to be in. 'Okay, I forgive you,' I said, trying not to sound too ironic.

He smiled a simple smile and began to untie me.

'Would you like a coffee?'

'Yes, and toast, please. Do you have any headache tablets? What time is it?'

Connor glanced at his fat gold watch. 'It's 2.30.'

'2.30? What day is it?'

'Friday. Friday afternoon.'

He looked away, seeming a little embarrassed.

Forgetting where I was, I asked about United.

'They won, I think.'

'You don't follow football?' I asked trying to warm the atmosphere a little.

'I think it's a stupid game played by stupid people. All those Gazza-types, earning too much money and letting the country down with their stupid antics abroad.'

He said country like a young tory at a party conference. The word connoting not pride or patriotism but ownership. 'They're just not English. Little explosions of self-righteous anger when they cannot get what they want. Their self-entitlement is just not English.'

My mind wandered to Gemma the waitress. Had she turned up? She would think I had stood her up. It probably didn't matter. My mind wandered again. As he turned his back to tidy away the rope, I was greatly tempted to hit him hard and to tie him up and to beat information out of him - any information. It wouldn't matter what he told me. It would be too unprofessional, I thought.

The room upstairs was much warmer. It thawed out all thoughts of violence. I swallowed two paracetamols, drank his freshly ground coffee and I ate his toast, all the time watching the waves roll into the horseshoe harbour.

'Tell me, who did you think I was when I climbed in through the kitchen window? You said you thought I was him.'

'Fish. I thought you were Fish. Rebecca said he would come looking for her here. She told me to provide him with a very physical reception.'

'Why did she think Fish would come here?'

'Rebecca's friend Sally told you she was here. She thought

you'd tell Fish, then Fish would come. My job was to convince Fish to stay away from Rebecca.'

How did Sally know I was working for Fish? Who told her? Did I tell her when I was tripping? What else did I tell her? Had I completely misjudged Sally? I was falling for her, and she was letting me fall deeper and deeper into something quite different. It didn't feel good to know that I had been betrayed by someone I thought really liked me, someone I was growing to like a lot.

'Rebecca told Sally to tell me she was here so that I would tell Fish?'

'Yes. That was the plan. Well, something like that.'

'You don't know what Fish looks like, so you thought I might be him?'

'Yes. Rebecca though you'd tell Fish. He'd come and I'd be waiting.'

'But you didn't answer the door when I knocked?'

'I was taking a shower. I knew you would come back. That is, I knew you would come back when I thought you were Fish. Rebecca told me that Fish is a very persistent man. He would not knock once and give up. I must admit, I was surprised when you climbed in through the kitchen window. I am really sorry that I hit you. I really mean it.'

He offered me his hand. I ignored it.

'And you imprisoned me.'

'I'm also sorry about that.'

What had Rebecca told Connor about Fish to make him act like this?

'I could report you to the police.' I knew I wouldn't. I would just accept it as an unfortunate aspect of the job.

He said he was sorry again and made more coffee.

I asked if I could use the phone. I phoned Andi and, without saying much in front of Connor, I asked her how things were. She had been very worried. She asked why I had broken our golden rule. We have a rule, golden, I suppose, about staying in contact with the office. Changed plans, new destinations, that sort of thing, we phone in to the office answering machine. Not a particularly sophisticated procedure but it makes us feel a little more secure, probably a false sense of security, but better than nothing. Andi got the idea from a film and thought it such a good idea, we've used it ever since. She asked if I was okay. I told her I was okay and would explain later.

After two cups of coffee, Connor began to talk freely about Rebecca. 'I tried to talk some sense into her. But it was no use. It was already too late. She told me about Fish. She also told me about the other one - Warner. That was better than her other scheme.'

I asked him what he was talking about. He explained Rebecca's plan to get herself infected with AIDS. I couldn't believe it. I thought of Guy. I thought of Fish and Warner. What kind of person is Rebecca Morney? Naive, dangerous, or mad?

I was still wondering if Connor, with or without Rebecca, had had anything to do with Warner's murder, when he told me about Rebecca's plan in a crazy matter-of-fact manner, without moral judgement. He was so obviously in love with her. They say love is blind. His love had torn out his eyes, leaving only dark hollow sockets. I almost felt sorry for him.

'He's dead, you know.'

'Who?'

'Warner. He's dead.'

'Already?' There was almost a hint of concern creeping into Connor's voice.

'No. Not AIDS. He was murdered. Someone blew the back of his head off with a shotgun.'

I regretted immediately the callousness of my description. Connor's treatment of me was infectious.

'He was murdered?' He sounded sincere. But some people can do sincerity with ease.

I nodded. 'Did you ever meet him?'

'No, why should I? I wasn't a student at Rebecca's stupid university.'

I was getting sick of Connor, the pub intellectual with a very expensive education. His parents should ask for their money back. I wondered whether or not to tell him that Warner wasn't HIV Positive. I decided against it.

Connor had hurt me, and I wanted to hurt him hard. But what was the point? I tried to dismiss all thought of taking vengeance. But the more he talked, the more he remained in front of me, the more the idea of vengeance grew. I had made a promise I knew I would not be able to keep.

Suddenly I had heard and seen enough. I hit him hard. Pointless or not, I hit him again, and then again. Taken by surprise his attempts to defend himself were in vain. I hit him until he collapsed into the corner of the room. He was moaning softly. Blood trickled from both his nose and mouth. Without speaking, I passed him my handkerchief and left.

I left by the front door. As I closed it I noticed the green MG sports car. I walked over to it and peered in through the windscreen. Inside was clean and tidy. I don't know what I expected to find. A shotgun and used cartridges? A confession? I resisted the temptation to damage the car.

Walking back to the car park I felt hollow inside. When I'd hit him, he'd become more than himself. He was more and I was less. Any satisfaction I'd derived in the name of vengeance had drained away very quickly. There was only an empty space where my vengeance had once crouched. There was even the possibility that I might vomit. I steadied myself against a stone wall. An old woman passed slowly. She gave me a look halfway between pity and fear. I tried to smile but only succeeded in producing a sullen grimace. She hurried on, undoubtedly thinking I was drunk.

My body ached everywhere, especially my head and shoulders.

I tentatively touched the back of my head. There was a large painful lump. I felt very tired. Thinking straight was a real effort. I wasn't even sure it was an effort worth making. I staggered on feeling very sorry for myself.

I stopped at a phone box just before the car park. Young school children were throwing stones in the river. They stopped when I stopped. As I pulled open the phone booth door, I smiled what I thought was a reassuring smile. They looked at me with great suspicion. I closed the door and phoned Andi's number. She answered after the second ring. This time I told her what had happened. We arranged to meet later.

I crossed the road, and I bought The Guardian. Manchester United 2 Southampton 1. I read the report quickly as I walked. I started the car and set off for Manchester. I'd expected to be clamped or there to be at least a ticket, but I found neither. As a long stay car park, it was true to its word.

I drove the car quickly out of the car park, still expecting an attendant to rush at me waving a wheel clamp. I turned away from the town and climbed the hill out of the valley. I would be in Manchester in a little over three hours.

As I crossed the moors, it began to rain. As the rain fell, the windscreen wipers beat out a steady rhythm of defiance. Very soon the rhythm was drumming out a question, repeatedly. Where is she? Where is she? Where is she? This wasn't helpful. I turned on the radio to drown it out. Radio 4. I was being told about an explorer who was increasingly concerned about the decreasing number of places to explore. I hated explorers. Rich people with nothing better to do. I flicked it to cassette mode. Hank Williams was singing 'Cold, Cold Heart.' It wasn't long before I was singing along. Perhaps shouting loudly would be a more accurate description. The rain was coming down hard, making visibility difficult.

After about two hours I could see the lights of Manchester sprawling across the valley below. It was more and more like looking at a map that was magically coming to life. So much promise mixed with so much pain. The thought came while I was trying hard not to think at all. Seeing the evidence of so many lives made me feel strangely alone. I was trying to impose a mental map on the lights: here was Hulme, there was Didsbury, here was Dumplington, there was Rusholme, here was Old Trafford, there was Maine Road. It was very hard to do. The more I tried, the more the lights resisted. My only certainty, but I wasn't certain at all, was that Rebecca Morney was somewhere out there. Was she hiding or was it just that I was not looking in the right places? I would soon be among these lights, weaving my way into Withington. Would I find her there, at last?

I stopped the car at the top of Lees Hall Crescent. It was 6.30. The journey had taken less than three hours. I parked a little way from Rebecca Morney's house. I walked cautiously through the drizzle. The lights gave the wet street a yellow glow. It was very quiet, except for the wind blowing yesterday's newspaper and fast-food wrappers from pavement to road. The quiet dance of litter and wind was briefly interrupted by a dog barking and then a door closing.

The house looked empty. There was no sign of a light anywhere. Another false trail? I walked quickly down the drive and around the back, still no sign of anyone home. I looked in through the kitchen window and then through the window of the back room. I saw no one. I returned to the front garden. I was becoming increasingly convinced that I was not going to find Rebecca Morney here. It was then, just as I was thinking what I might do with the rest of the evening, that I noticed that the front door was slightly open. Suddenly I wished Andi was with me. I didn't need her to hold my hand. I wanted her with me to talk me out of what I was about to do. I hesitated and then slowly pushed open the front door. I listened for a moment. No sound.

I was just about to enter the hallway when Guy banged

into me hard. All the pain of my time with Connor suddenly thundered an unwelcome return. My back crashed into the door. I grabbed at him, but he was too quick. He was gone before I could even think of chasing him. I had only caught a brief glimpse of his face, but I was sure I saw tears.

I stepped inside the hall. I steadied myself, swallowing the pain that Guy had revived. I listened again. My experiences in Whitby had made me cautious. There was no sound of anyone else in the house. I closed the door behind me.

The front room was empty. So were the back room and the kitchen. I quietly climbed the stairs. The bathroom was empty, as was the first bedroom. Rebecca was in the second bedroom. She was lying on the bed. Her body was pale and still. I tried hard to focus. I knew it was the little things, the things that appeared to have no significance, which were often the real clues to solving a crime.

Her beautiful moist eyes were frozen, staring blankly at nothing in particular. Her head leaned to one side, almost touching her left shoulder. Her paleness made the red of the bed cover seem dark and deep. There was a little stream of vomit that had formed a snake-like pattern down the front of her blue and white shirt. I leaned forward. Yes, I was right, the smell of bitter almonds. She had been poisoned with cyanide.

The smell of vomit and bitter almonds was invading my nostrils. I pulled my head away. I took two steps backwards. Agatha Christie entered my head. It was as if I had stepped by mistake into a literary death. A death or murder, I asked myself. Had Guy done this? I knew I would have to tell the police.

I did what I knew I had no need to do. I felt for her pulse. There was absolutely no sign of life. I touched her left leg, low down, as far away from the vomit as seemed possible. I touched my own left arm. Her body was not much colder than mine. The body cools by about two to five degrees Fahrenheit each hour. There was no sign of rigour mortis. It might not be science, but my guess was that she had been dead for no more than a couple of hours.

I realised then that I had only ever seen her still: first frozen in a photograph, now lifeless on a big expensive bed. These thoughts came quickly. But this was my second dead body. Only the second dead body I had ever seen. Of course, I had always known that my work might introduce me to death, but I still wasn't prepared for this. I wanted to turn and run. The vomit, the smell, the pale dead flesh. Struggling against myself, I gripped the back of a chair. I stared at the vomit crawling down her blue and white shirt and then at her pale lifeless flesh. I felt like I was being sucked in. Nausea was overwhelming me. I thought I was going to pass out. I gripped the chair as firmly as I could. My knuckles were as pale as Rebecca Morney's body. I turned away from her and violently wretched. But I wasn't sick. My eyes watered. I didn't know if I was crying or not. But someone should cry. Someone would cry. Someone had already cried.

My throat was drying up rapidly. I sucked in air as best I could. The silence seemed to stretch out and grab me by the shoulders. I blew out air and tried to control my breathing. My eyes were on the point of ignition. I steadied myself to examine the scene more carefully. I knew that there would be times when I would close my eyes and see Rebecca Morney's pale and lifeless body, and the little snake of vomit. My head would become like a cinema that randomly screens the details of Rebecca Morney's death scene. Never showing who had done it, only what he or she had done. At such times I would try hard to fix my imagination on the photograph I had been given by Fish. Controlling my dreams would be much harder. They would begin as mumbles and end as a deafening roar.

Once back in my car, I locked the doors. I started the car and went in search of a phone booth. I drove passed the house. I took a left down Ladybarn Lane, then left again on to Moseley Road and right on to Wilmslow Road. The first phone was vandalised. At the second, I called the police. I gave the details quickly, including Guy, refusing to leave my own name.

I had started feeling sick. I parked the car next to Platt Fields. The vomit came as I was climbing out. It was not a thin snake but a crashing torrent, splashing down my shirt and on to the pavement and my boots. I steadied myself and reached back into the car for a bottle of mineral water. I poured some into my mouth and washed it around, then spat it out. I did this three times. Then I took a long drink. I felt a little better. I gathered grass and leaves from the hedgerow and wiped the vomit from my boots. I got back in the car, and I froze. An hour went by, perhaps longer. I sat frozen. My head buzzed with the death scene, the pale dead body, the snake of vomit, the smell of bitter almonds, but most of all, my contribution to it all. I sat frozen, forced to see, and smell it all again, while a violent cross-examination echoed in my head.

I had looked at her body for less than a minute, but it was long enough for the visual details to tattoo themselves on my imagination. I knew then that I would witness this scene again and again.

Two hours, perhaps longer, went by. I had completely lost track of time. The world had seemed very quiet. The only interruption had been the wail of a police siren. I listened as the siren came out of the distance, passed close by, and then away again. I started the engine and drove to my apartment.

Chapter Eighteen

Saturday morning.

Fish phoned at 8.34. He sounded very cold and distant. But his tone was demanding and authoritative. He said we needed to meet. He proposed 11.00 in my office. I agreed, knowing I had very little choice.

Fish arrived at the AndTom Detective Agency at 11.03. I had been nervously looking at my watch for about fifteen minutes. For the first ten minutes or so he hardly uttered a word. He was obviously distraught. He sat down. He got up and walked around the office. He sat down again. He did this several times. I sat behind my desk, and I observed. I knew - at least I thought I knew - I would only get the whole story when Fish was ready to tell it.

It was an unusually hot day for May. We were both sweating, visibly. The window was wide open, but the air was very still. I listened to the rise and fall of the noise coming from the street below. I did something I rarely do. I tried to decipher the noises, separate them into their component parts. Individual voices formed and faded. The occasional phrase almost made sense. I thought I heard the words to whole sentences. But I couldn't be sure I wasn't imposing sense on the waves of noise coming up from below and entering the room. I heard a young woman shout. It sounded like a call of joyous recognition. But again, I couldn't be certain. Since building work had begun across the road, it was no longer possible to be sure of individual sounds.

Too often they lost their individual identity in the general noise of construction. I wanted to move to the window and connect the voices to the faces and the figures down below, but I was worried it would slow down the coming of the moment when Fish would speak.

Then he began. 'I used to spend a great deal of time looking at old photographs of myself. I suppose I was trying to make some sense of the distance between myself now and myself then. It was reassuring in a strange sort of way. I could make promises to my old self, knowing that my new self could keep these promises. I could also explain what I had achieved. I did this often.'

Fish was struggling to find a context in which to situate his crime.

'Now I worry that soon they'll be no one to reassure my old photographs. There can be no reassurance anymore. She's made that an absolute fact. I would have once condemned such a statement as hopelessly empiricist and essentialist. She has even changed that – even that.'

The heat seemed more oppressive than ever now. Fish loosened his tie and undid the top button on his shirt. He next removed his brown sports jacket. It was then that I first saw the revolver bulging from the inside pocket of his jacket. Fish placed the jacket on the filing cabinet. He carefully placed it so as to ensure the gun's invisibility. I wondered if Fish knew that I knew he had a gun. I pretended that nothing had changed. I waited for more. I tried not to listen to the noise outside, down below. It seemed to be getting louder, demanding attention. Fish shuffled his body slightly and started again.

'I faked the suicide. I wiped my fingerprints from the shotgun and laid Warner's hands on it. I'd seen it done in a TV cop show. It was not difficult to do; too easy, really. Well, that's how it seemed at first. The police were much smarter than I had anticipated. But it doesn't matter now. It probably didn't matter then.'

I quizzed him gently about the details. 'But why the CD playing on repeat? Was that you?'

'Yes.' Fish explained, almost smiling, 'It was a semiotic joke. Warner had told Ester Smith, probably while he was drunk, maudlin drunk, that he had died that day he'd come home early to discover his wife fucking a neighbour with Gorecki's Symphony No 3 playing as background music. I just thought he might like the same music at his actual death. Everything's in the semiotic details.'

I inwardly shuddered. I recalled the poster in Smith's office, **Idle Talk Costs Lives**. Of course, she wasn't to blame. But her information had added something to the circumstances of Warner's death. If she gave me a hard time again, perhaps I'd tell her. If the newspaper reports had mentioned the music, she would probably know already. Perhaps without the opportunity of this excess of signification Fish might have been unable to do it. Perhaps Warner might still be alive. Perhaps. But very unlikely.

'Did he tell you about his marriage?'

I didn't answer. I just waited, offering a brief but encouraging smile and a movement of my hand.

'He told Ester that he knew his wife had been promiscuous before they met but he had believed that she had been so because she lacked something that he could give her. The kind of hopeless optimism that, well, you know what I mean. In the end he was forced to concede that she just liked sex with lots of different men. His presence made not the slightest difference. In fact, it may have even encouraged it. It was this knowledge which really ended their marriage.'

He was laughing again, a gentle laughter, perhaps thinking of his own part in the downfall of Warner's marriage. I wondered.

'I suppose you want to know the facts? The facts!' He laughed. It was a disturbing kind of laugh that seemed to come to his body and not from out of it.

'Well, I had an affair with Rebecca. I ended the affair. I met her in China of all places. I was a Visiting Professor, and she was an exchange student. After a lecture I gave, she stayed behind to say hello. I had no idea who she was. But she explained that she had attended my lectures in her first year at Manchester. I was quite amazed. We were both from the same institution, and we were meeting for the first time in an institution 6,000 miles from home. I didn't know she would be there; she didn't know I would be there. I have absolutely nothing to do with all that exchange student shit. But we now had a bond. I explained the situation to my Chinese hosts. They suggested that Rebecca come out with us for a meal. That's how it started. We ate together, we drank rice spirit together, and then we slept together. It should have ended there, but it continued for the rest of my stay in China.'

He rubbed his right hand across the desk. I waited. He bit his lower lip.

'We walked on the Great Wall, and we walked on the city walls of Nanjing and Xi'an. We looked in the guidebooks and then we did what the guidebooks told us to do. We were living in a travel utopia of two. China made me feel very rich and I spent my wealth in the pursuit of happiness. We stayed in the Peace Hotel in Shanghai, walked around the Bund and the Nanjing Road. In Beijing we visited Tiananmen Square, the Forbidden City, and the Temple of Heaven. We walked together across the beautiful campus at Wuhan University. We visited the Terracotta Army and Banpo in Xi'an. Qingdao was the best of all. We did everything there. Remember, Tom, I gave you a box of Tsingtao beer. A sort of semiotic clue.

I nodded. 'It's good beer,' I said.

'Hainan was very hot, and the sea was mostly too rough for swimming. But we had a great time.'

He talked for a while as if in a dream. He was somewhere else. Maybe back on the Great Wall or drinking beer in the Tsingtao factory or holding hands down by the river in Shanghai.

'We travelled down the Yangtze River to the Three Gorges in an old tin steamer. Three days to get there and back. We loved it. One beautiful evening, drinking rice spirit, I told her the story of Marlowe's journey to meet Kurtz. Later the same evening we made love on the deck beneath the stars. A working boat passed by, and we had to lie together very still so as not to be caught in its lights.'

Fish's words stopped and his mouth slowly formed into a smile. He was almost laughing when he began speaking again. 'When we flew from Beijing to Shanghai, we changed planes at Qingdao. Instead of hanging around the airport, we went to the Tsingtao Beer Festival and then continued on to Shanghai. Doing things like that was so symptomatic of our time together in China.'

He continued to calmly recite the details of where he and Rebecca had travelled together for almost another ten or so minutes. He then sat quietly for a few moments.

'I had been back in Manchester for about six weeks when Rebecca returned. She came to my office and made it very clear that she expected us to continue what we had been doing in China. Maybe, to her, it was a perfectly reasonable expectation? I don't know. But Manchester isn't China, as I explained. She wouldn't listen. She didn't want it to end. She just wouldn't let go. She was so very insistent. In the end, it drove her a little insane. Certainly, what she did was insane. She deliberately contacted the HIV virus in order to kill herself, to kill me, to kill my pregnant wife and to kill our future child. I call that insane. Don't you?'

I didn't answer.

'She told me she slept with Warner to get AIDS. Can you believe that? She then contrived to sleep with me again. I slept with Rebecca, not knowing about Warner, thinking only it would let her down easy. You probably don't believe that. I don't believe it. She waited about a month, to be sure I had slept with my wife, then she told me I should take an AIDS test and that it was almost certain that my wife and I were now HIV Positive. She didn't know that my wife was pregnant, but she might as well have said, and your future child will also die.'

I thought of another poster, the one on the wall above the desk where Guy had rolled a joint. Rebecca Morney's poster, a quotation from her favourite children's story: ***You can do all kinds of things if you need to enough.*** But to do this, it was hard to believe.

'At first, I thought she was just mad at me. Making it all up just to get back at me. I told her so. But she soon convinced me that what she had said was true. She told me about the counselling, the blood test, and the death-sentence results. She told me with such glee in her voice. It was unbearable. She was unbearable. I exploded and threatened to kill her. I took the test. She was right. I was HIV Positive. My wife would be. No doubt. Our child would be born with a death sentence. How was I supposed to deal with that?'

My mind raced. Had Warner lied to me about his health? Perhaps he was not as innocent as he had represented himself to be? Perhaps the real innocent was Tom Renfield?

'I decided I would kill her. I followed her to a friend's house in Rusholme. As she crossed Redruth Street, I drove my car at her. I thought I'd killed her. I learned later I had only injured her leg. She was hardly hurt at all. She then disappeared. I made certain inquiries. But all to no avail. That's when I came to you, Tom. I paid you to find her. I paid you to find her so that I could kill her. When you told me she had slept with Warner, I killed him as the original source of the virus. I had not believed that part of her story. But you found out the truth for me.

'When you discovered Rebecca's whereabouts, I went to the address and killed her. I went to the house, to the address you gave me. Without wishing to sound too melodramatic, I knew my fate: my grief lies onward and my joy behind.'

He was beginning to sound like a mad man. Was he really threatening me, warning me? Or was he just playing, just being Professor Brian Fish, the man who would now never be Director of School? I hadn't cared before about his directorship, but the thought that it was now impossible terrified me.

'I had made up my mind. She could say what she liked, but

it would not change a thing. How with this rage shall beauty hold a plea, whose action is no stronger than a flower? I went to the house in the distraction of a maddening fever. I sought her out in my madness. Desire is death. Past all cure, I was past care. I left the house knowing that all men are bad, and in their badness reign. Don't feel too bad, Tom. You know, I couldn't have done it without you.'

Fish got up and walked across to the filing cabinet. He removed the gun from his jacket pocket, returned to his chair, sat down and then placed the gun on the table. We made eye contact. He lifted the gun from the table, only a few inches, but just enough to warn me against anger or heroics. Luckily, I felt neither.

'Shaw says somewhere, I think it's in one of the plays, maybe Major Barbara? I can't remember. It doesn't matter. What he says is 'You have learnt something. That always feels at first as if you had lost something.' Is that what it feels like, Tom?'

I didn't answer. There was no point.

'Killing her has not changed a thing. Do you realise that? Not one little thing, Tom.'

I remained motionless. I knew that the time to respond had not yet come.

'I guess I thought it would. I still shake. I still clench my fist. I will still die. Oh, for fuck's sake, why am I telling you all this? Why am I sitting here quoting Shakespeare and Shaw?'

A terrible thought crept over me. He was telling me all this because he guessed that I already knew enough of it to point the police in his direction. I was the only one who suspected Fish, kill me and who would think to connect him to the deaths of Warner and Rebecca? I was hoping even more now, desperately hoping, that Andi would not come back to the office. In the face of so much death, we were mere amateurs. Suddenly being a store detective looked more than exciting enough.

Fish smiled a mirthless smile.

'Isn't that what they always say? I don't know why I'm telling you all this. Is my case in any way unique? Is it unusually messy or strange?'

I remained motionless. I wanted only to hear the full confession and then draw the case to a close without, hopefully, another dead body.

'I lied about China. True we did spend time together there. But it was not our first meeting. I first noticed Rebecca at a research seminar. It was a very good session. I made my usual contribution. It started as a question and quickly became a statement about my latest piece of research. The speaker had seen and heard it all before. But Rebecca was genuinely impressed. She more or less told me so in the pub afterwards. She was a very attractive girl. I mean, she is, was, a very attractive young woman. I was very flattered, naturally.

'No. I wasn't flattered. The way she talked made it fairly clear that she hadn't really understood the paper or my contribution. I wasn't flattered. I was sexually attracted. She was a very attractive girl and I wanted to fuck her. You've seen her eyes. My mistress's eyes are raven black. These words were never so true.'

He smiled. 'You have seen only a photograph. You should have seen her eyes when wide with desire. Raven black.'

I could remember only frozen eyes staring blankly at nothing, a snake crawling down her blue and white shirt and the suffocating smell of vomit and bitter almonds. I calmed down and with relief recalled the dark and misty eyes staring out from the photograph. I remembered the revelations I'd heard and seen in Staithes. I was certain now that her eyes articulated sadness, a strange sadness, a sort of mad desperation. Desperation articulated as beauty.

'Temporarily anchored in the bay where all men ride. Enjoyed no sooner but despised straight. Actually, that's not true. I wish it had been that simple. I really do. I first noticed her when she came for a tutorial on *The Waste Land*. I told her what she needed to know, what she needed to do, to scrape a low 2.2. This seemed to be both the limit of her ambition and the extent of her intellectual ability. I'd helped her the way I would any student of her ability and commitment. But unlike the other students, she didn't mumble a reluctant thank you and leave. She got up from her chair. If I close my eyes, I can still see her doing it.'

Fish closed his eyes. His grip tightened on the gun. She rose from her chair and shook my hand. 'Thank you for all your time, Professor Fish. You've been most helpful. I really appreciate it.'

Fish paused again. This time his eyes remained open. 'You're probably thinking that I was hooked by mere politeness. It wasn't the politeness. Really, I don't give a shit whether students are polite or not. I judge them by the signs of their intelligence. Rebecca wasn't particularly intelligent. I did not see anything to indicate that she might be capable of anything more than a low 2.2. She wasn't even particularly polite. No, it wasn't that. When she rose from her chair and shook my hand and thanked me for my help, it wasn't politeness. Fuck, it's difficult to explain. When I try, I sound like the narrator from one of those romantic novels we teach our students to despise.'

He closed his eyes again. When he opened them, there was almost the hint of tears. His eyes blinked gently to prevent any tears becoming visible.

'I know what most students think of me. You were a student of mine. You know what I mean. Well, I don't give a shit what they say. I don't give a fuck what they think. Most of them don't even think, anyway. They certainly don't think significant thoughts. If they do, I've not seen the evidence. Anyway, whatever they think or don't think, whether it's right or wrong, it was different with Rebecca. *I* was different with Rebecca. It wasn't her, it was me. She made me like myself more. That's at the heart of it. It's not liking or loving someone else. It's someone else making you like or love yourself.'

Fish stopped again. He was tuning in to a private soundtrack. Perhaps he was also listening to the traffic down below. After a few minutes he began again. 'I'm contracted to write a book on love for Edinburgh University Press. The provisional title is *Literature and the Subject of Love*. It'll be my ninth book. Signing the contract alone was enough to secure my directorship.'

Fish paused, suddenly distracted. Perhaps reflecting on his success, current and forthcoming.

'*Literature and the Subject of Love*. It is . . . it was going to be my best book. My masterpiece. I was going to dedicate it to Rebecca,' he said, as he began to laugh in a very uncharitable way. 'But that won't happen. Not now. The book won't get written now. You're probably wondering why I'm telling you all this. What possible relevance can there be in the fact that my ninth book will never get written?'

I was beginning to wonder about the significance of Fish's book on love. In other circumstances, I'd have expected him to spend time talking about his success, to expand and to elaborate endlessly, but not now.

'I've written the first chapter. That's all I'll write. It's a general discussion of love articulated around a critical analysis of *Sonnet 138*. I wrote it as a direct result of Rebecca. Without our relationship, there wouldn't be a chapter. And now because of our relationship there will not be a book.'

He remained silent for a moment.

'I've loved her all my life. Even before I knew her, I loved the possibility of her. I have always been in love with that possibility. She made that possibility flesh. She gave form to something of which I had always dreamed. This seemed especially true when we were together in China. I don't normally like holding hands. But we walked along the Bund hand-in-hand looking at the river and the colonial architecture. I felt so happy I could have died there and then. It would have been better if we had both died then and there.

'When she came to my office and expected Manchester to be China, she should have known it was impossible. She should have known that I was a different person in Manchester. I had to be a different person.'

Fish was silent again. He was shaking slightly. I imagined the grip he might have on the gun. His mouth opened again. Many words came but they only formed a short sentence. 'Do you remember Sonnet 138?'

I nodded, but without much conviction. The truth was, I can never remember the numbers. But I would always remember Fish's phrasing: 'Do you remember?' rather than 'Do you know?' I wasn't being asked if I 'knew' the sonnet, only if I 'remembered' it. Presumably, Fish could only think of my literary knowledge as something that he had himself planted all those fruitful years ago in lectures and seminars. Fish was making me paranoid again. He didn't need a metal phallic prop to do that. Words were more than enough. I realised fully for the first time that I was scared. Really scared. A dark knowledge was beginning to grow inside me that I might be experiencing the final moments of my life. The feeling was overwhelming me, making it difficult to concentrate, to think straight, to even think at all. I took a deep breath and tried hard to focus on everything around me, determined not to let myself go, let myself float loose.

Suddenly Fish's words anchored me; pinned me to the floor. At first I didn't understand. Then I did. I knew I would be able to hold on. Listen and focus and I would get through this. Fish adopted his seminar manner. There was some reassurance here. With great authority, he announced, 'Let me remind you:

When my love swears that she is made of truth
I do believe her, though I know she lies,
That she might think me some untutor'd youth
Unlearned in the world's false subtleties.
Thus vainly thinking that she thinks me young,
Although she knows my days are past the best,
Simply I credit her false-speaking tongue:
On both sides thus is simple truth suppress'd.

But wherefore says she not she is unjust?
But wherefore say not I that I am old?
O, love's best habit is in seeming trust,
And age in love loves not to have years told:
Therefore I lie with her, and she with me,
And in our faults by lies we flatter'd be.'

Fish articulated Shakespeare's words in a voice resonate with understanding. There was a beautiful clarity about his enunciation. It was like listening to the performance of a truly great song for the first time. For the duration of the sonnet, I was somewhere else, no longer in an airless room with a mad man and a gun.

On the surface, it seemed clear why these words might express something of Fish's understanding of his relationship with Rebecca. But I knew, knowing Fish, that there would be more. He would explain, no doubt. I wouldn't try to stop him. The more it became like a tutorial, I figured, the less chance there was of Fish using the gun.

'I don't really see the connection between you, Rebecca and the sonnet?'

'The flattery of lies. The truth that only lies can tell. The prison house which self-deception makes for those who demand fulfilment of love's promise.' He spoke as if to someone else in the room. 'The worst was this: my love was my decay.'

He continued to ignore my question. 'The impossibility of love. Love is the name we give to that which we can never experience. The paradox of love is that it exists only as a disguised desire for a return to something we have never actually experienced. Shakespeare's pun - 'love's best habit' - to suggest both custom and clothing and thus to imply the possibility of an essential nakedness or naturalness recoverable underneath, is absolutely central to the myth of love: the belief that we can, with the right person, get beneath and behind custom and clothing to discover the real 'me' through the real 'you.' But discovery is really an attempt at recovery. But what we seek to recover cannot be recovered, because it never existed in the first place. Hence the impossibility of love.'

Fish was now in full flow. He was standing at the lectern at an international conference. Perhaps he was back in Shanghai? He talked a lot about being imprisoned by a reckless impulse, and how he would give anything to turn back the tapping fingers of time. He repeated in different ways the idea that what others call making love was making him dead. It had already made others dead. He talked like this for over an hour. Then he stopped. He said nothing for almost five minutes. He just sat still, his eyes occasionally closed and his hand gripping the gun he had placed so carefully on the table between us.

I wondered if Fish's understanding of why Rebecca had deliberately sought to become HIV Positive was in fact accurate. Given access to the information I had gathered, Fish might find the question of motivation a little more complicated than he now thought it to be. Fish had paid for this information. Why was I so reluctant to give Fish what he had paid for?

'Love Story said, 'Love is never having to say you're sorry.' But love is really the promise of never having to speak. It is the illusion of completeness. Love promises to make us whole again. That's why we invest so much in it. That's also why it can hurt so much. Disappointment in love can at times be too much to bear. It's all an illusion because it can never happen. Yet we say it happens all the time. It's a necessary illusion. An illusion to live by, like religion or politics.

'The sonnet takes us to the heart of this illusion: love is about lying with and lying to another person. Perhaps love is the greatest lie of all?'

He lifted up the gun and pointed it at the window. He touched the barrel with the index finger of his left hand. He let it linger there, tenderly rubbing against the cold metal. I realised that I had never seen a gun so close before. It looked both hard and beautiful. The sunlight from the window sparkled upon its solidity, making it become liquid, almost.

'I've posted a letter to my wife. She should get it on Monday. I didn't leave a note in case she found it before I have done what I have to do. Anyway, the letter explains what has happened and begs for her forgiveness. I'm telling you all this because you deserve to know. You've probably already worked out some of this for yourself. You must talk to her if she needs to know more or if she doesn't understand what I've said.'

I tried hard not to shake my head. The thought horrified me. But it did seem to mean that he did not plan to kill me. The relief that should have come, did not come. I couldn't shake my head because I was fearful that if I did it would trigger off my whole body shaking.

Fish suddenly lifted the gun with his right hand. He held it up for examination. Here was a 'text' more than worthy of very serious consideration.

'My relationship with Rebecca was much more complicated than you will ever know. I could explain but you wouldn't understand. There isn't enough time. She opened a door, and I walked through. As Huxley says, the man who comes back through the door is never the same man. That is how it was with me.'

I nodded, but before I could speak he held up his left arm to warn against interruption. 'When I was with her I felt like I was starting again. I don't mean that I felt like I was young again. I felt like I was young in a way I had never been young. I had never been young before. I was always too busy doing something else to be young. Now I could be young. Life owes me this. It fucking owes me this. It owes me Shanghai, the Bund, the Peace Hotel, the Nanjing Road. It's not too much to ask.'

He banged the handle of the gun hard against the table. I don't know why but I really tried not to show fear. But I was frightened. Very frightened. Fish was on the edge of hysteria.

If he banged the gun again like that it might go off accidentally. He calmed down just as suddenly as he had erupted.

He now held the gun with both hands. His finger on the trigger and the barrel pointing at me. 'You saw her dead body? Right, Tom?'

I nodded, trying to remain calm.

'I should have beaten her to death. I should have strangled her. I should have stabbed her. But, as I think you know, I poisoned her with cyanide. Did that surprise you, Tom? It shouldn't have done. Ours was a literary relationship, therefore a literary death was the most appropriate. I could never hurt her, at least not in that way. The car was a mistake. I was angry. I panicked. I wanted a death that would be quick and relatively painless. I thought she deserved that. I arrived. I told her I was sorry. It was true, I was genuinely sorry. She made drinks: two cups of green tea. I watched her remove the beautiful tea leaves from a red tin box she had carried all the way from China. I was thinking about the day I bought it for her as I spiked her tea with cyanide.

The signs and symptoms vary with dosage. The recipient may become anxious, excited, their breathing may become rapid, followed by feeling drowsy, a headache and nausea. Eventually drowsiness turns in to coma. The dose I put in her tea spared her these symptoms. She went into a coma within seconds of her first mouthful of Chinese tea. She was dead in less than a minute.'

Fish's account of how he had murdered Rebecca made it sound so clean and so necessary. Perhaps he really believed that was how it was. All I could see were frozen eyes staring blankly at nothing and a snake crawling down her blue and white shirt, and the suffocating smell of vomit and bitter almonds.

'I sat by her side for a very long time. I stared at her, and I remembered our time together in China. Without at first realising it, I began to talk to her about our room in the Peace Hotel.'

'We were so wholly one, I had not thought that we could die apart. The words repeated in my head as I watched her body on the bed. But the seminar room came between us. Edna St Vincent Millay stood there as a poet to be explained. Birds should drop, and fish should drown.'

He was silent for a few moments. 'Words that should have been a reminder, an instruction, allowed me to hesitate and delay. I should have had the courage to die with her.'

He visibly gripped the gun more tightly.

'I've had the same dream, most nights for the past two weeks or so. Rebecca and I are running together along an outstandingly beautiful beach, probably Sanya on Hainan, when suddenly the sea changes into an enormous upright mirror. We stop to look at our reflections and begin to undress, each watching the other's reflection in the mirror. And then it ends, always the same. Once all my clothes are off I vanish, leaving Rebecca alone, admiring her own body, oblivious to the fact that I am no longer there.'

He was quiet for a moment. When he began to speak again his tone had lightened. He sounded less desperate.

'That's how it feels. I'm unpacking all the things I've kept hidden these past few months. It feels good. Every time I heard talk of a murder on the TV, I felt guilty and wondered whether I was involved, whether I was the person who did it. Talking to you about what I've really done I no longer feel like a sponge for other people's crimes, for other people's guilt. It's a great feeling of relief. You have been a great help, Tom.'

I cringed at his last sentence. I knew it was a sentence, much longer than I would get for murder. I felt the sudden rush of a mad heroism. If he's going to do it, let him do it now. Then he lifted the gun slowly and pointed it very deliberately at me, as if responding to my changed sense of security. I felt sweat on my back. There was a pounding in my head. Heroism was draining away rapidly. I tried to ask a question. I tried not to beg. My voice sounded strange. Fear had tightened my vocal cords. Something had changed. I knew very powerfully what I suppose I had always known - I was very afraid to die.

A small bird, fragile in the breeze, landed on the outside window ledge. It was oblivious to the human drama coming to its conclusion inside. It pecked at something for a few brief seconds and then it was gone. I wanted to follow the bird, out of the window and into the pale blue sky. Even to fall from the sky like Icarus would be better than this.

Fish smiled at me. There was a certain resignation is his manner. He was bringing something to its conclusion. It was as if this was the ending he had always envisaged. There is a terrible beauty to be derived from enacting what has always been inevitable - enacting with good grace what one cannot escape. He reached into his inside pocket and withdrew a light brown pencil with a pink ring around the top.

'Don't worry,' he said. 'This is not your payment. I noticed that you collect pencils.'

I felt a little embarrassed.

'It's from the Peace Hotel in Shanghai. It's said to be the most famous hotel in China. I thought it would be a good addition to your collection.'

I tried to thank him, but the words would not come He placed the pencil on the desk. I thought I saw a small smile on his face. But I could not be sure. Perhaps he was back there again?

He reached again into an inside pocket and withdrew a dark brown envelope. He handed it to me. 'This should cover your fee and expenses. There is no need to count it now,' he said, unnecessarily.

I took it from him and placed it down on the desk. It all seemed irrelevant, inappropriate, something blocking the natural flow of things. I picked it up and put it in the table drawer.

'All these things will be lost soon. No one will ever remember Rebecca and I walking together by the Huangpu River in Shanghai. This and the many other things we did together will be lost as if they had never happened. There is one last thing you can do for me, Tom. Please remember what I have told you of my time in China with Rebecca. Tom, please remember what I told you.'

I could not speak, I just nodded.

Fish had stopped talking, filling his mouth instead with the barrel of the gun. I was shaking involuntarily. He smiled with his eyes and then closed them, and his finger squeezed the trigger. He blew off the back of his head in an explosion of blood and noise.

He lifted the gun. Its long phallic barrel glittered in a shaft of sunshine flickering into the afternoon gloom of the office. He placed the barrel gently in his mouth and he blew off the back of his head.

He opened his mouth, placed the tip of the barrel inside and he pulled the trigger. There followed an explosion of light and sound and blood. Fish's body jerked violently. The gun banged hard against the table and then the floor.

I froze. I remained frozen in that moment for what seemed like a very long time. I saw the action again and again and again. I feared I was trapped, forever, to watch Fish shoot himself - again and again; my own movie theatre, playing the same film over and over again.

The sound of a car door slamming in the street below brought me to my senses. Without thinking I walked to the window. The street was very busy in the spring sunshine. A young woman, pushing a pram, was joking with her friend. A little boy was skipping. Another boy was throwing a football high into the air. Two small girls were walking holding hands and singing a recent hit. A man and woman stood in the entrance to the Peveril of the Peak. Everything was just so normal, just so very normal.

I was still sitting opposite Professor Brian Fish when Andi arrived.

I was on my third bottle of beer when the police arrived. They examined Fish's body, made some phone calls, and then I explained what had happened. I answered all their questions, more or less. Their irritation became palpable. It quickly turned to aggression and abuse.

'Private pricks.'

'Can we talk somewhere else?' I said gesturing towards Fish's body.

The second officer answered. 'For definite. This is now a crime scene. Forensic people are on the way. You will have to leave. You'll be told when you can return. Don't make any plans to travel.'

'You private pricks make me sick. You get paid for this shit. What's the world coming to?' added the second officer. 'You orchestrate a fucking mess and then you get paid, while we are expected to just arrive and clean up the fucking mess you've made.'

They say you learn from your mistakes. The question I fell asleep asking myself was do more mistakes equal more learning? If an answer had come, I had forgotten it by the time I awoke the next morning.

Chapter Nineteen

Monday morning.

At the office, Andi and I sat together by the window drinking freshly ground coffee. It was beautiful May morning in Manchester. The police had allowed us back in late Saturday night. We had more or less cleaned up all the blood by early Sunday morning. In the afternoon, we had gone to Old Trafford to watch United play Coventry. It hadn't been much of a game - United 0 Coventry 0 - but it was a tremendous celebration. United were champions for the second year in succession. The possibility of the double was only a week away. I was even beginning to believe what Andi had been telling me all season, that it was the start of a glorious new era.

United's success and the anticipation of more, however, had failed to lift my spirits. According to Fish's account, I was an accomplice to murder. But it was over. There had been a conclusion, but it had hardly been a successful case. Four people dead. Most of the time spent chasing clues. Four people dead and I hadn't really detected anything. The solution to the mystery had finally been gifted to me. And four people were dead.

I checked the answering machine. Once I had heard the message, I wished I hadn't bothered. There was just one message. Sally's voice started loud and angry, probably amplified by alcohol. She blamed me for Rebecca's murder. She told me she had made it very clear to the police the extent of my role in Rebecca's death. She raged and raged, hardly taking a breath in a five-minute onslaught, littered with expletives, shouting and tears. I think I understood how she was feeling. I didn't feel that good myself. I wondered how much of her anger was a response to her own sense of guilt. If she had told me the truth, Fish would never have found Rebecca. Although she had made it very clear that I should never contact her again, I wondered if I should try just one phone call. I wanted to do it, but somehow I knew I never would.

I didn't need to be told by Sally that I had made a mess of things. The evidence of the case's resolution still stained the office carpet. Four people dead. I felt I was responsible for at least one death. Maybe two. I had lied to Fish because I suspected him. It was a barely articulated suspicion, but it had been enough to make me lie. I had lied to him to protect Rebecca. Sally had lied to me to protect Rebecca. She had sent me to Whitby to allow her friend to escape. Together our lies had conspired to produce the conditions for Rebecca's murder. Sally's plan had failed horribly. I cannot even say I had a plan.

I had spent some time early Sunday morning writing my report; pointless, really, as Fish had been my only client. With no one to present it to, I would just file it in the office cabinet. I was putting the final touches to the report, little thinking that it would need a postscript, when there was a knock on the office door. I was half-expecting the police. I had been very stupid. It was obvious that naming Guy would lead to Guy naming me, even before Sally got around to giving them my name. They would ask lots of questions. They had promised me as much in our rather unpleasant meeting on Saturday evening. I might face a charge of withholding evidence. It seemed like nothing in the circumstances. They had not been too impressed with my role in two murders and two suicides. You call yourself a detective. Fucking private detectives. Fucking amateurs. Paid fucking amateurs, at that.

I opened the office door with a sense of relief mixed with deflation. The visitor was Trefor Trelawny. It was the first time I had seen him since our chance meeting following what the late

Bill Warner had referred to as Dr Ester Smith's famous lecture on Lacan and detective fiction. It seemed like such a long time ago.

Trelawny said hello and sat down. He was wearing a brown checked jacket, cream shirt, pale green trousers, and brown shoes. As he made himself comfortable, he adjusted his dark brown tie.

Had he come to buy me the drink he had promised and to talk about detective fiction? His manner, although polite, made it clear that this was not the case. His manner also made it clear that he had been drinking. I figured he must be here in connection with Fish's death.

It became clear very quickly that Trelawny was unaware of the full circumstances of his late colleague's death. I felt no particular compulsion to enlighten him. He eventually got to the point. 'I believe you were doing some work for Brian Fish. So sad, so sad,' he added.

'Yes. Fish was my client,' I said, coldly.

Trelawny looked uneasy, unsure of how to proceed. He undid his top button and pulled down his tie a few inches. He hesitated for a moment, cleared his throat, and then plunged straight in. 'Can I ask you to disclose the nature of the work?'

'I can't disclose information about a client. Alive or dead, I'm afraid,' I said, trying not to sound too rude. I immediately wished I hadn't added 'alive or dead.' 'The ethics of the job forbid such disclosures, I'm afraid.'

'I suppose you must be wondering why I have come here today, to ask you to tell me things about the investigation you were carrying out for Brian Fish?'

He sounded like he was about to begin a lecture on the influence of wind in the poetry of Shelley. I felt obliged to interrupt him. I had grown sick of being lectured. At least this looked like a lecture without a gun.

'As a matter of fact, I am curious. Do you want to tell me why you've come here today to ask me to disclose the nature of the investigation I was doing for Brian Fish?'

He became thoughtful. Suddenly he was smiling. 'I suppose that's why I am here, to get information and to make a confession of sorts. Can I call you Tom?'

I was also smiling. I wasn't sure why. I nodded.

'Please call me Trefor,' he said, pushing his tie further down his front. His jacket would be off next.

I don't normally do it, but I offered him a drink. Another drink, I suppose. He said yes and I opened two bottles of Tsingtao. It somehow seemed appropriate.

'You were a good student, Tom, one of our successes. Can I ask, have you ever read *Origin of Species* by Charles Darwin?'

'Not all of it. I've read bits of it. I have a copy at home,' I said, suddenly wondering where I had put the book. 'Why do you ask?'

'Darwin says that discovering the truth of his theory and then committing it to print was like confessing a murder. It's a funny thing, but as I walked across town today to visit your office, I couldn't stop thinking about what Darwin had said. It suddenly struck me as enormously profound. I suppose I had already decided that if you were not forthcoming with the information I sought, I would make do with a confession. Before I start, will you answer one question?'

'It depends,' I said.

'Was I, in anyway, part of the investigation?'

'No, you were not part of the investigation. Not even in a small way.'

He smiled and took a long drink from his bottle of Chinese beer. 'It doesn't really matter, I suppose. I'll tell you anyway. If I tell my story, it might help you tell me what I need to know,' he said, hopefully.

He walked over to the window, studied the scene below and then turned to face me. He suddenly looked like a man in need of another drink. I removed a couple more bottles of Tsingtao from the fridge. There were not many left and it seemed right to share what was left with one of Fish's colleagues.

I handed him a bottle. He reached for it and said thank you. 'Here's to China,' I said, raising the bottle to my mouth.

'Yes, here's to China,' he replied, looking unnecessarily grateful.

'Have you ever been?'

'Where?'

'China.'

'No, but I would like to go. Fish went. He told anyone who'd listen what a fabulous time he'd had.'

'He told me about it too. It did sound like a good time. I would like to go myself. Maybe someday,' I said, dreamily, images of Rebecca and Fish moving rapidly through my head. I saw them in Shanghai and Beijing, Qingdao and Sanya, Nanjing, and Wuhan. It was like watching the end of a very sad film.

I got two more bottles from the fridge, and we talked a little more about China. Putting the third bottle to his lips he said: 'I'm in love with Mrs Fish. Geraldine and I have been in love for almost two years. The question I want you to answer is this: Did Fish hire you to find out if Geraldine and I were having an affair?'

'No, he didn't. I told you, you were not in any way a part of the investigation. Not even in a small way,' I said, wondering about Trelawny and I drinking Fish's beer. 'He hired me for quite a different purpose.'

'That story you told me about looking for a missing student, it was true?'

I hesitated, thinking again how I'd helped Fish murder that missing student. 'Yes.' I hesitated. 'Well, sort of.'

After another mouthful of Chinese beer: 'About six months ago I had a test for the HIV virus. The result was positive. More than positive, I've got full-blown AIDS. I'm dying of AIDS.'

I emptied my third bottle. 'Does Mrs Fish know?'

'I have never been able to tell her. I have been too frightened that it would end our relationship.'

I wondered about the baby. Did Trelawny know about the

baby? He hadn't mentioned it. If he didn't know, what did that say about his relationship with Mrs Fish? Then the thought occurred: whose baby?

I remembered seeing Trelawny with a woman in the rain outside the Handsome Sailor from Naples. The woman must have been Mrs Fish. If I had known that at the time, would it have made any difference to my investigation? I wanted to ask him about it, but instead I opened the last two bottles of Tsingtao.

'I think you should go to Mrs Fish. She will receive a letter in the post today that may further distress her. Your presence might help.'

'A letter from you?'

Trelawny looked as if he was on the verge of becoming angry. I didn't want to be involved in a drunken brawl, especially when I was myself still too sober. I remained calm. 'No, not from me. The letter is from her husband, Professor Fish. He told me on Saturday that he'd sent it.'

'I thought you said . . .?' He stopped and swallowed another mouthful of Chinese beer. 'What does the letter say?'

Trelawny was no longer on the verge of anger, instead he now looked a little uneasy.

'I don't know. Go to Mrs Fish, she may have the letter by now. She'll need someone with her.'

'Did Fish know? You know, about Geraldine and I?'

I wanted to tell the truth as I knew it, but something made me respond with less openness. Perhaps I wanted to punish Trelawny. Punish him just a little. 'I don't know. The letter should make that clear. You should go to see her. I really think you should.'

'You probably think I'm a real shit. I sleep with a colleague's wife. And if that's not bad enough, I infect her with a killer virus. Moreover, I don't tell her that I've sentenced her to death.'

'I'm not paid to judge you,' I said, trying hard not to sound too self-righteous.

'Paid or not, you will judge me, you are judging me now. You sit behind your table, and you judge me. I'm not proud of what I've done. I fell in love, I had unprotected sex with a strange woman on a drunken night out a very long time before I fell in love with Geraldine, and I sentenced to death the only woman I have ever truly loved. Don't you think I have been judged enough already? I don't need your judgement. If I were Warner I could take comfort in the certain fact that Geraldine and I would meet again on God's golden shore. But unlike Warner, I don't believe in any of that crap. All I know is that I have sentenced to death the only woman I have ever truly loved. I can't imagine a more grave and severe judgement. Can you?'

I couldn't, so I remained silent. Trelawny stood up and without saying another word he left, leaving the door open behind him. I rose and closed the door. I walked to the window and gazed down at Great Bridgewater Street. Across the road, the Manchester International Concert Hall was taking a recognisable shape. I thought again about the rumour I had heard that they were thinking of making a canal connection, linking the hall with the Rochdale Canal. This would surely mean the demolition of the offices of four textile and clothing firms and the AndTom Detective Agency. It was perhaps the right time to think about starting again somewhere else.

Thoughts of moving were interrupted by the sight of Trelawny crossing the road and turning left into Chepstow Street. Instead of continuing on into the city centre, he turned right and into the Peveril of the Peak. It had probably been his last place of call before coming to the office. I smiled, thinking that Fish's letter would make easier reading after three or four more pints. I guessed this was Trelawny's opinion too. Mrs Fish would probably know where to find him.

Four people dead. Soon the figure might be seven. But the case was over, hardly a great success, but over, nevertheless. Fish had paid in full. Under normal circumstances the money would have been something to celebrate. But the need to earn money was no longer quite so pressing. First thing that morning I had received a phone call from the estate agent informing me that they had found a buyer for my mother's house.

The money would keep the AndTom Detective Agency afloat for another couple of years or so. We'd been thinking of buying a second-hand Ford Transit for surveillance work. We couldn't decide whether or not we needed it. What was certainly needed was some investment in the new surveillance technology of detective work. We would certainly use some of the money to do that.

I needed another drink. I needed a big weekend. I closed up the office and left the building. I walked past the Peveril of the Peak. I did not want to see Trelawny again. Not so soon, anyway. I walked aimlessly. After walking for about twenty minutes, I found myself in Salford. I was outside a small pub in a busy street. I went inside with the intention of getting very drunk. I talked only to the barmaid and only to order drinks.

After two or three hours I walked out into the rain. I was very drunk. A man in his late twenties was selling the Big Issue. He smiled at me and held up his magazines wrapped in plastic. Water dripped from above the doorway in which he stood. His hair was so wet it seemed as if it were painted on. He tried to shake the rain from his face, coughed and then asked if I wanted to buy a magazine. I said yes and handed him a fiver. He fumbled in his pocket for change. I told him not to bother. He coughed again, smiled and said, 'The rain is so heavy today, one could almost drown.'

I walked away from the pub, heading for my apartment and my bed. It began to rain more heavily. Everywhere lights were coming on. In the blur of light and rain I thought I could see Fish's last words, 'There is one last thing you can do for me, Tom. Please remember what I have told you of my time in China with Rebecca. Tom, please remember what I told you.'

Epilogue

I woke early. Forgetting breakfast, I got in my car and drove to toward the university. Remembering breakfast, I stopped at La Lluvia en España and ordered Chorizo Breakfast Eggs. I washed it down with a glass of sparkling water and a strong black coffee.

I needed to think about what had happened. Almost unconsciously, I drove to Rusholme.

Parking the car next to Platt Fields, I listened as a police siren gave way to a song on the radio. I listened and I heard myself singing the words. Singing along as if these were my words; as if these words were a commentary on everything that I had done and seen; a commentary on everything that had gone wrong; a commentary on every fatal mistake I had made. Baffled by my own incompetence, I wondered at what I had really done. I sang loudly, desperately, and opened the window to allow the rain to join with my performance. From Platt Fields I was accompanied by the struggling whines and whistles of a lone starling.

I saw the badly painted sky, dripping out of shape, and then I saw a man, as liquid as the water running down the windscreen. He walked by and almost stopped, looking at me singing along, alone, loudly to a song on the radio. I turned off the car's engine and the music stopped. I was trying not to think, trying not to remember, when the man returned. This time he was on the driver's side. He leaned in through the open window, and in a sudden flash of light, turning quickly from white to grey, I felt a slash that burst open my throat. My eyes widened and then closed. My heart was banging like an unlocked door in the wind. I tried to undo my seat belt. I tried to stand up. But I could not do very much at all. I was shaking. I was wet. I was gasping for air. I was a drowning man.

As the credits began to roll on Tom Renfield's life, the man leaned in again and turned on the car radio. It played Johnny Nash singing, 'I Can See Clearly Now.' The song continued to the end of the credits. The man listened, nodding along to the insistent bass line, and then he walked off down Platt Lane.

The only sounds that remained were the struggling whines and whistles of a lone starling.

FIND US ON SOCIAL MEDIA

@northodoxpress

@northodoxpressofficial

@northodoxpress

@northodoxpress

www.northodox.co.uk